Minno

James Barlog

BAK
BOOKS
San Diego, California

Printed in the United States

Library of Congress Cataloging in publication data on file

ISBN : 978-0-9831453-0-1

To Cory,

His brilliant creativity has been invaluable in creating the fascinating characters and wonderful world depicted in this story.

1

The faded yellow Volvo station wagon clattered along a dappled road, bottlenecking a dozen irate drivers in its wake. In the passenger seat, Minno white-knuckled a manila envelope while staring out the windshield at a weathered brick Blue Lake Middle School. At thirteen, changing schools had to be about the most terrifying thing to face. Her mind churned uneasily; her stomach twisted up into stranglehold knots. Would Blue Lake be any different from her last school?

"Grampa, you're straying ..."

Whop!

"Over the curb," Minno pointed out as politely as possible.

Her Grandpa Esri jerked the steering wheel hard left, but the right front tire had already crested the curb, bouncing them off squeaking, threadbare seats.

"Again," she added to punctuate her remark.

"Oh," Esri eeked out, working the wheel the opposite way through knobby hands. A painful screech warned he had reached the wheel's limit of rotation. He succeeded, however, in bringing the vehicle back onto the pavement.

Minno sunk lower into her seat, hoping her grandfather's inept arrival had somehow escaped the students milling outside the school. She already struggled with two things that set her at odds with her peers. She hated both her name, which of course, brought grief at every new encounter, and her changing eye color. Minno's irises had the oddest propensity to alter their color as sunlight played off them. Some claimed she had chameleon eyes. Others, the meaner ones, called her a freak. The irises alternated between a deep-ocean blue and a stunning verdant green, depending on how light struck them. In stark contrast, they switched to a shimmering silver in the twilight.

Otherwise, Minno stood no taller than her peers, nor was she any shorter. She detested piercings and body art, though her grandpa would never allow such anyway. Her chestnut hair she kept cut moderately short, rough and wild, as did most girls her age. And her fashions she carefully selected to blend in amongst her classmates. The less she stuck out, the more easily she escaped their uncensored ridicule. Her name alone brought enough of that.

Minno held an unfocused gaze on the handful of geeky sixth graders playing kick ball who turned to stare at her. To be noticed by sixth graders was the last thing Minno wished on her first day. As if the whole 'changing schools' thing weren't embarrassing enough. Minno avoided eye contact by casting her eyes downward. She just knew they were snickering at her.

"We're here," her grandpa announced triumphantly. His overgrown bushy white eyebrows curled upward with his smile, while the morning breeze jostled strands of his wispy white hair. His face clearly claimed success while simultaneously pleading innocence for his latest driving offense.

Minno glanced at the collection of students loitering on the grass. She had to quiet the exploding urge to slam her foot over her grandpa's on the gas peddle and roar away from there. Like it or not, she would have to exit the car and make her way past them to reach the main doors.

Her mouth turned to cotton. She tried to swallow as she watched a tight cluster of eighth-grade boys, all in skewed ball caps, black rapper t-shirts and drooping pants, claim the stairs before the main doors.

This was going to be more difficult than even she imagined.

"Avoid eye contact," she breathed. "Say nothing, no matter what they do," she breathed in again. "And whatever happens, just keep walking," she mumbled in a long final breath.

"Perhaps I should ..." Grandpa Esri started, shutting the engine down.

"No!" Minno shot back sharply. "I'm fine. I can do this alone," she added a second later more calmly.

She loaded her reddish-tan leather bag over her shoulder. Her forced smile hid an encyclopedia of adolescent insecurities. Everyone would have laughed had she walked up the path with her seventy-two-year-old grandfather, whose torturously slow pace would have only prolonged her agony.

She clutched the broken door handle, pumping it repeatedly like a well pump to persuade it to engage the lock mechanism and release the door. The screeching hinge made her skin crawl.

"Everything will be just fine, you'll see," Esri offered as a departing thought. His smile washed away her tension—but only for that moment.

Minno's smile wilted as quickly as it came.

She could do this. She just had to focus on what she told herself.

She left the car wearing black jeans, an equally black t-shirt and a black hair band, all coordinated specifically so as not to allow her to stand out in the crowd. And she never looked back at her grandfather. She fully expected him to remain idling at the curb until she entered the building. Looking back at him revealed fear and uncertainty, something she must never allow any of them to see.

A commotion on the stairs erupted. Taunting and yelling drew all eyes to the double doors—and off Minno.

She paused.

BLAM!

The red kick ball careened off her head, bounding down the walk with its hollow twang. Minno spun with fire in her eyes. Her jaw tightened.

Laughing, the sixth-graders scattered.

"Creepy little trolls," she scowled under her breath. The only thing she hated more than sixth graders was ... she couldn't think of anything she hated more at the moment. Wait, sixth-grade boys. They were annoying, juvenile, craving constant attention. Next year she'd go on to high school, and she'd never have to deal with middle-schoolers again.

The mean-spirited taunting at the doors called her back. Minno turned to witness a girl her age with short, jet black hair struggling to reach a suspended notebook, which a lean blond boy held hostage at arm's length. He towered over the poor girl by at least six inches.

"Oops, too slow," he chuckled, snapping his arm away to keep the notebook out of reach.

Minno's fist tightened on her bag strap. Anger swelled into her throat. The exchange between the two was nothing more than pure bullying.

Another boy, with black-rimmed glasses resting on piglet cheeks, and a matching porky belly that bulged beneath a two-tone orange horizontally stripped shirt, punched the books from the tormented girl's hand. School papers scattered.

The bell's clatter discharged the moment, causing the onlookers to crash like the running of the bulls through the double doors.

Minno squatted to help retrieve splayed papers.

"Hi ... Hailey," Minno offered, extracting the name from a 'D' test, "I'm new ...."

Fighting back tears, Hailey crushed her papers into an angry fist before dashing into the building. In a moment, Hailey was gone, never once turning back to thank Minno for her kindness.

Minno returned to her feet, alone on the stairs. Her first exchange had not gone so well. And she would probably hate this school as much as she had hated her last two.

Inside in the main corridor, Minno contorted this way and that, weaving through the current of students all surging against her. A few boys checked her out, but most either bumped her aside or narrowly missed her, without so much as a second glance.

Minno finally located the office near the center of the main hall. Someone from behind bumped her rudely into the glass. She sucked in a deep breath before grasping the cold, lifeless doorknob. Her brain screamed for her to turn and run. But she swallowed the fear and pushed the door open. She had done this enough to know the drill and exactly what would be expected of her.

A prominent black plastic nameplate on the counter read MS. KILEY.

Minno handed over her envelope without waiting to be told. She watched as Ms. Kiley perused her previous schools' records, offering one of those phony puckered-raisin smiles. Minno knew for a fact there was nothing to produce the elder woman's facade, since Minno mostly kept to herself, never disrupted a class and always turned in her work on time, even if most never achieved better than a C for her efforts. It wasn't that she was dumb; her previous teachers all agreed Minno just didn't apply herself. At least that's what they told her grandfather each time he dutifully attended the parents' night conferences at her last schools.

"Third school this year," Kiley said, gazing at Minno over pearl-frame glasses. "Your parents circus people?"

Kiley thought she was being funny.

"Yes, ma'am. I mean, no ma'am. I live with my grandfather," Minno offered politely, though the meanness of Ms. Kiley's remark tore into her heart. If that old biddy with wrinkled drooping jowls and flapping upper arms knew the truth, she'd be apologizing all over herself for that remark.

"One of those," witch Kiley responded. She set Minno's school records aside while the bitter old woman took up a classroom assignment sheet she kept nearby. Minno concluded that witch Kiley most likely lived alone with her two cats, which were probably rescues. Minno had only been there a few minutes, but she already concluded the woman must be evil.

"Let's add you to McCully's eighth grade home room, shall we? That's room fourteen, just down the hall from here on the left."

Witch Kiley slid a class schedule and a hall pass across the counter.

All eyes in room fourteen turned when Minno entered. She tried to swallow. *This was the moment of truth.* A lump of dread choked off her breathing. She wanted with all her heart to spin about and run until she was so far away, she couldn't even see the wretched town of Blue

Lake. But her feet remained frozen. Her hands trembled as she limply offered her paperwork to Mr. McCully's expectant hand.

Balding, beady-eyed McCully, in turn, faked a smile.

"Class, let's welcome ..." he paused, seeking the name on the papers.

The moment seemed interminable. Then McCully opened his mouth to speak. Here it comes!

"Minno? Is that correct?" he said with such surprise that the entire class exploded into raucous laughter.

Minno attempted to hide her embarrassment, though her face had flushed ruby red. She struggled for a way to recover.

"It's M-i-n-n-o, not the fish," Minno spelled out, hoping to establish a clear, and somewhat respectable, distinction. But it didn't matter.

"Welcome, Minno, not the fish!" her new classmates chimed together as if they had rehearsed it for the past hour.

Minno wanted to sit down right there on the floor and cry. She avoided eye contact with her fellow students, fearing that in itself would spark real tears. Instead she swallowed, choked down the embarrassment and scanned across the eighteen students. Her eyes met Hailey's, who, it turned out, was the only one *not* laughing at her.

"Find a seat, Minno," McCully said.

Minno's eyes strayed over to the mean boy in the orange shirt who had knocked Hailey's books from her hand on the stairs. With a wicked smile, he offered her the vacant chair in front of him. Then relief washed over Minno upon seeing Hailey's kind green eyes motioning to the empty chair beside her. In that one instant their friendship began. Without uttering a word, Hailey had connected with her. Something in Hailey's smile let Minno know she was going to be all right.

2

"You've *never* been able to speak?" Minno asked, trying to constrain her surprise. She and Hailey sat facing each other at the 'outcast' table, a rotted fringe outdoor lunch table bordering tightly-packed pines along the edge of the school campus. They sat alone, as no other student would even approach them. It seemed Minno had befriended Blue Lake Middle School's leper, which was probably fine, since she also felt like an outcast. The afternoon sun warmed them against the cool westerly breeze coming off the ocean a dozen miles distant.

While Minno spoke, Hailey texted on her outdated cell phone. Her nimble fingers moved with the efficacy of someone who could easily bang out a hundred words a minute.

EVRY1 HATES ME BORN MUTE Minno read off her cell phone screen.

"Him?" Minno asked. Her nod indicated an eighth-grader, whose shoulder-length straw-colored hair partially covered his face. He sat three tables away with two friends involved in a belching contest, and it seemed, he couldn't pry his eyes off Minno.

BAND GEEK came back to her phone.

Minno's interest dulled after reading the words. Besides, he really wasn't that cute anyway ... with his braces. Okay, he really was cute

8

enough. But if Hailey proclaimed him a geek, she'd take her new friend's word at face value until she could determine otherwise.

Hailey crinkled her nose—her way of conveying distaste. Minno quickly realized she needed to read Hailey's face as much as the text on her cell phone screen. The subtle context of what Hailey communicated came through in her expressions. The cell phone offered mere words.

Plop!

Bird dung splattered Minno's fingers.

"Aaaaggghhh!"

She squirmed right, using a napkin to clean her fingers. She prayed none would land on her head. That would be a disaster! Now she understood why the other students relegated outcasts to *this* table.

Minno texted as best she could, being quite inept at the process, since she had no friends to text to anyway most of the time. Then she realized she should just speak to Hailey. Minno's finger dexterity was clunky at best.

Hailey fingered Minno's shoulder bag on the table beside them. She mouthed 'leather.' Minno saw envy on her new friend's face.

"I think so. My grampa gave it to me for my birthday last year."

Minno dismissed the wishful glint in Hailey's eye. And she could understand why. Hailey wore thrift-store markdowns: threadbare, ripped jeans and a worn, stained shirt. But, those could actually be considered fashion diva in Blue Lake, for all Minno knew. Hailey carried no bag, rather she pulled her cell phone from her pocket when they sat down to eat.

It had only been a few hours, but Minno felt a growing kinship to her new friend. It was as if the Cosmos had brought them together on the steps of Blue Lake Middle School. Maybe, just maybe, life at this school wouldn't be so disastrous after all.

As Minno waited while Hailey texted, another boy, tall and lean like a gangly basketball player, with a bashful grin that held her eyes captive, slowed his stride intentionally as he passed. He made no attempt to disguise those blue, probing eyes languishing over her, sending goose flesh up her arms.

"B-W-O-B?" Minno said, reading her cell phone with Hailey's latest text.

Minno stared, totally confused.

Crash!

The boy slammed into a banged-up wire-mesh trash receptacle chained to a post a few feet from their table. The basket clamored left, while the boy stumbled right, his face hiding his agony. But he turned askance, so Minno wouldn't see his grimace and his tearing eyes.

"I'm okay!" he chimed, pasting on a phony smile to mask the pain flooding his brain.

"What's B-W-O-B?"

BORN WITHOUT BRAIN came back a minute later.

The school bell's dull clank ended lunch. Both girls wished they could spend more time chatting, even though Hailey could only chat with her fingers, which she did as adroitly as most other girls babbled.

HANG OUT AFTR? MEET@BUS, Minno read as she found her next class.

All the trepidation she endured from the time she awoke this morning until she sat across from Hailey at the lunch table had vanished. For the first time that day Minno smiled as she strolled to her physical sciences classroom.

3

Hailey threaded her way through students spilling out the doors toward two outdated buses lining the curb. She frowned when she saw the battered pickup parked behind the buses.

Daryl. Mean evil Daryl.

Her pace turned sluggish as if her feet had become cement blocks. On her approach, Daryl's obnoxious snore grizzled out the open windows of the rusted vehicle waiting for her. Hailey swallowed the acid backing up into her throat at the very thought of him sitting there.

Daryl hated everything, and never hesitated to let everyone know exactly how he felt about anything to anyone foolish enough to engage him in conversation. He literally expelled whatever popped into his brain with complete disregard for how his words might hurt their recipients.

Hailey crept silently to the pickup window. She had to hope he remained asleep long enough for her to sneak away. She was relieved when Daryl kept snoring. Quickly, she scribbled a note that she tossed in. It landed on his mostly-empty pint bottle of Jack Daniels Tennessee whiskey. Daryl considered himself a connoisseur of fine beverages. That's because his lunches usually came from tipping a bottle. But not those cheap rut-gut whiskey bottles, as he would say. He had *refined* drunkard tastes.

Easing silently away, Hailey spotted Minno strolling up the walk.

"Did you see the fish eyes on that new girl when she was coming out of the bathroom?" an overfed eighth-grade girl said to her companion as they approached the buses.

"Yeah, like, I heard her name's, like, Sardine or something, like, weird like that," the other girl replied.

Neither realized 'that new girl' was behind them and within range of their words. Nor did they witness the pain in Minno's eyes as she struggled to keep their remarks from stabbing into her heart.

"I don't have fish eyes, you fat little ..." Minno blurted out.

Hailey snared Minno's elbow, steering her away before the girls could retaliate. Very unwise to provoke a confrontation on your first day at school. Hailey had learned that from painful firsthand experience.

"Hey, what stinks? Oh, it's Minno not the fish," creepy piglet boy in orange cajoled, laughing hysterically at his own joke. His belly quivered when he chuckled.

Hailey spun, ready to fight. She had endured about all she could take from that creep Wilbert.

But now it became Minno's turn to offer restraint. She placed her hand on Hailey's forearm to indicate she must show the same control she had advocated for her friend. Best to just let these things pass unchallenged.

"Shut up, Hailey," piglet boy Wilbert said in response.

"I just ignore 'em," Minno offered. Her words seemed to douse the fire in Hailey's eyes.

The girls boarded the second bus, watching the doors close before piglet boy could board. They both smiled at him as the bus pulled away to a screaming Wilbert.

Twenty bouncing and banging minutes later, the bus screeched to a stop on a rural road a little more than six miles from the school. A row of three battered mailboxes greeted the girls on their departure. Minno exited first with Hailey tagging behind.

"How long have you lived in Blue Lake?" Minno asked.

Hailey flashed three fingers.

"Years? That long," Minno said, surprised. Three years is a torturous eternity when you're unliked and unwelcome.

They crested the grassy rise on an unpaved winding driveway. At the end of the snaking drive, a quaint A-frame clapboard cottage with worn blue curtains on the windows came into view. Before it, a field of dried out grass stalks flowed like ocean waves in the breeze.

"Wait here until I clear it with my grandfather," Minno said before bounding ahead to the porch and through the screen door.

"Grampa, I'm home," she called out, though it seemed unnecessary. Esri stood ten feet away across the single room at the sink slicing peeled potatoes for their dinner.

"I see you survived your first day," he said. He set his knife aside before coming around with his proud paternal smile.

"You were right. It wasn't so bad."

"A grandfather, he knows these things."

"When's dinner?" Minno asked, rummaging through a cupboard for a snack. "I made a new friend."

"You did! Let me guess." Esri placed a wrinkled hand to his weathered brow as if to think very diligently.

"She's about your size, I'd say. She has black hair, much darker than yours, and is that ... yes, the cutest dimple on her right cheek."

"How could you ..."

Esri indicated the front door.

Through the screen, Hailey peered in like a lost puppy, admiring what she saw. She entered as soon as Minno turned to her.

"This is Hailey. She can't talk. Is it okay if she stays for dinner?"

"I think that's a fine idea. It's not often we have the pleasure of entertaining Minno's friends. But remember your chores, young lady."

"Grampa, we've never entertained a friend. Come on, Hailey."

Outside behind the cottage, while Esri bridled a drooping dappled mare in a makeshift corral, Minno led Hailey into the field of high grass.

WHAT R WE DOIN? Minno read off her cell phone when it chimed.

"Looking for a plant. It has large brown leaves and red veins," Minno said without taking her eyes off the ground.

WHY came back a moment later.

Minno abruptly abandoned her search to dash back to the cottage, where she mounted the mare. But she didn't ride it like someone would normally ride a horse; instead, she lay flat on her belly on the beast's back, clinging to wooden pegs strapped as handholds that Esri had secured to the mare's sides.

As the old mare picked up speed, Minno closed her eyes tightly and held on, praying she would survive her training. The mare attacked a section of shin-high picket fence, leaping over it handily.

"Very good, Minno," Esri said, "But you can open your eyes now."

"They're open," she claimed, knowing she was a bad liar.

Minno opened her eyes to the astonishment of having already passed the fence.

Hailey applauded, though she didn't exactly know why.

"Would you like to try?" Esri asked Hailey. She stood beside him.

Hailey shook her head. As much as she loved animals, she had never ridden a horse and was apprehensive of being on one of them.

While Esri returned the horse to its makeshift corral, Minno led Hailey back into the field. After a couple dozen paces, Minno took up a fairly straight fallen tree branch with a four-foot span. She measured it carefully across her hands.

Hailey tugged Minno's arm to snare her attention, wanting to understand what was happening. She got her answer when she turned to find Esri with a tree branch of equal length across his hands.

Without hesitation he attacked.

Hailey dove out of the way as Minno stepped in to block Esri's assault. Then she launched a clanking counterattack of her own. The two fought back and forth as if imitating a Stars Wars light sabre fight scene. When Esri lunged for Minno, she sidestepped him, using her limb to take Esri off balance at the knees. Tumbling, Esri promptly surrendered.

"Excellent, child, but mind your footing, can't attack when your butt's holding down the ground."

"And that, young apprentice, always provides a view of the world unsuitable for a victor," Minno said, mimicking Esri's British accent.

"Precisely. Wait, I don't sound that stuffy, do I?"

Both returned their sticks into the field and trekked back to the cottage.

"Remember, everything around you . . ." Esri started.

"Can be used for good, or for evil," Minno finished.

"You decide. For your greatest powers are right inside there," Esri said, indicating Minno's brain and heart. "Use them wisely, and they will serve you well."

Minno's cell phone chimed in a new text message.

THESE R CHORES? Minno read. She smiled.

"Wash up before sitting at the table," Esri yelled to the girls as they dashed ahead into the cottage. Seeing Minno's smile warmed Esri's heart. For too long she had no one but him. She needed a friend, and maybe, just maybe, now she had found one.

Finally it was time to eat. Both girls were famished from their time in the field behind the cottage. The three gathered around a small circular oaken table for dinner, one that had never seated more than two in the past.

Hailey filled her head with the aroma of the milky stew before her. Steam wafted out of the bowl. Hailey placed her hands in her lap when she noticed Minno waiting while Esri served up his bowl. The richness of the aroma swam inside Hailey's head, testing her patience. She just knew this was going to be something she would relish. It certainly surpassed the all-too-regular peanut butter and jelly sandwich she received as her dinner at her house. As a matter of fact, she had trouble remembering the last time she actually had heated food for dinner. It was cold generic cereal for breakfast, peanut butter and jelly for lunch, and most often, peanut butter and jelly for dinner. Sometimes she got a treat—bologna. She guessed those days were the times when they felt really sorry for her. Except for the one time on her birthday when she got a real meal for dinner, one that actually required cooking before serving.

Once Esri sat down, he carefully unfolded his napkin across his lap. Only then did Minno fill her spoon and begin to eat. Hailey wasted not a moment longer to get that first full steaming spoonful into her mouth.

"You do like rabbit, don't you?" Esri asked Hailey with his toothy smile.

Hailey stopped. Was he serious? His words seemed so measured, so carefully delivered. He couldn't be serious? It was already inside her mouth! She stared at Esri in disbelief. Then she looked to Minno. Neither smiled; neither were laughing. They *were* joking, right? They had to be. Were they actually ...

Hailey couldn't swallow, nor could she find a polite way to evacuate her mouth. The thought of eating rabbit sent her insides convulsing.

"It's chicken," Minno jibbed after swallowing hers.

Esri raised an eyebrow while he smiled his 'got-you' smile.

Hailey at last swallowed. She was so hungry she emptied her bowl in less than three minutes, enjoying every single bite of her dinner.

"I surmise that means you enjoyed our stew?" Esri asked of her.

Hailey smiled, shook her head jovially yes.

"Wonderful," he added.

Following Minno's lead, Hailey set her bowl into the sink beside Minno's, then both girls moved the ten feet to enter the living room, where they settled down cross-legged on the floor before the fireplace. They waited while Esri popped popcorn, which he placed into two bowls before proceeding into the living room, where he settled into a rocking chair. From there he took up an oversized leather-bound book he removed from a shelf with at least fifty other books. The large book totally consumed his lap.

TV? Minno read on her cell phone. She shook her head no, so as to remain quiet while Esri began.

"Where were we?"

"The ten-years war where the king fell in defeat," Minno offered.

"Ah, yes. After a hundred years of peace, war now ravaged the land. No creature in Ambrosia was safe from the bitter conflict. Hatred and fear bred throughout the valleys into the villages and into the mountains. Craveaux rallied the people against their king, who they believed had become vile and corrupt. But it was not the king all in Ambrosia had to fear, it was Craveaux. He had lied and betrayed those that trusted him. He said he would bring peace. Instead, he brought terror, darkness and despair."

Here Esri paused to trace his index finger along the page. He wanted to be certain he had not missed anything.

The girls munched their popcorn while waiting for Esri to resume.

"Alone, Desrilian descended the mountain to confront the evil Craveaux. He knew they had been betrayed. He knew he must find a way to free those Craveaux had imprisoned. This would be the first—and the last—time the two would be face to face, and Desrilian couldn't know what to expect. But he was prepared to fight to the death to save his brethren. Everyone, save the Palladins themselves, was depending on him. It was Craveaux who unseated the king to seize the kingdom for himself. But no one had any inkling of Craveaux's true intent once he held the power. From his newly usurped throne, Craveaux turned the Palladins against all the creatures in the land."

Esri stopped when Minno's cell phone chimed.

"What did she say?" he asked.

"Nothing," Minno offered after checking her cell phone. "Go on."

"Under Craveaux's rule, the Palladins began stealing magic wherever they could. Their raids grew more daring, more ruthless with each passing month, threatening to exterminate all creatures. During the darkest days of their fight for survival, Desrilian foresaw their destiny in the conjurings of a crystal vision. And from that moment on, he knew he must risk everything to find a way to change what he had seen."

"What did he see?" Minno asked with rapt excitement.

The cell phone chime broke the spell that held the cottage.

Esri pressed back into his rocking chair. The drama of the moment had evaporated.

"*That* shall be for another night. Do you believe in magic, Hailey?"

Hailey shook her head with such conviction that there left no room for debate. No one actually believed in magic. It was all just trickery meant to separate people from their possessions.

"Perhaps we've read enough for tonight. It is time your friend got home."

As Esri lowered the book, Hailey noticed that the characters on the pages were not letters, nor were they numbers. Rather they were strange indecipherable scripts. Yet Esri read them as fluidly as if they were English.

Hailey nudged Minno with greater insistence.

Her cell phoned chimed. U ASK HIM?

"I will," Minno whispered, hoping her grandfather wouldn't hear. But of course, he did.

"You will what?" he queried.

"Can Hailey sleep over? Please, oh, please," Minno blurted.

"Oh. I, but her parents must ... I don't ..."

Esri stopped himself. Disappointment flooded the girls' faces. He could see his response tore into their hearts.

"Perhaps, in honor of Minno's new friendship and successfully completing her first day at her new school, a sleepover to celebrate is indeed in order. If," and here Esri paused for effect, "Hailey's parents say it's all right."

Hailey turned her phone around so Esri could read the screen.

WHATEVER, came in response to Hailey's earlier text asking to sleep over at her friend's house.

The girls sprang to their feet, dancing about the room hand in hand.

"Your parents are way cool," Minno said as she twirled with Hailey. Hailey stopped, shook her head and texted.

THEYRE DRUNK FOSTERS ALL THEY CARE ABOUT IS THE MONEY

Minno choked on Hailey's reply. Her heart sank as the words worked their way into her brain. She knew exactly what being without parents felt like, but she had no idea what it was like to live in a foster home, to be with people who didn't love nor care about you the way her grandfather did.

Esri joined the girls in celebration in the center of the room.

"But sadly, it is time for young princess Minno and young princess Hailey to scamper off to bed. They must get their beauty sleep, so they will look fresh and radiant in the morning's first light."

Esri went to a table lamp on a round table situated in the corner of the room. There, he held his hand above the lamp shade, then gently blew across it, as if extinguishing a candle. The light bulb went out on his gesture.

Hailey's eyes went wide with disbelief.

Minno led Hailey up the rickety ladder to an open loft bedroom covering part of the living room.

While sitting on the bed, they texted under the faint illumination of a small light on Minno's bedside table. Beside the lamp a pewter picture frame held a black and white photo of a man and woman in an endearing embrace. However, upon closer inspection, Hailey quickly realized the photo was the stock photo that came inside the frame at purchase, as it had the price stamped in the lower right corner.

WHAT WAS YR GRANDPA READING?? came over Minno's cell.

"You wouldn't understand," Minno said.

Hailey texted again.

THANX 4 BEIN MY FRIEND. WHAT HAPPENED 2 YR PARENTS?

"They died ... in a car crash. I was a baby. I never knew them," Minno revealed. She realized Hailey had now become the first person to know her secret.

IM SORRY.

Minno noticed the silver locket suspended around Hailey's neck. Hailey opened it to show her the small faded photograph inside.

"Your mother?"

Hailey nodded. Her hand clutched the locket tightly.

"What happened to her?"

Hailey didn't text. She just tucked the locket back inside her shirt.

"What about your father?"

PRISON Hailey texted back. Sadness consumed her face. Then she smiled.

I LIKE YR GRANDPA

"We better go to bed now, or he's gonna get upset with us."

Somehow Hailey could never picture Minno's grandpa being angry. Hailey texted furiously trying to get everything typed in before the light went out. Minno's cell phone chimed.

"I wish I never had to go home again," Minno read off her cell phone. "I'm glad we're friends," she added on her own.

Hailey held her hand up. Minno high-fived her.

"You can come here whenever you want," Minno offered.

Hailey smiled.

"I mean it. We can hang out here, do things together."

Minno stopped herself. Her words sounded desperate.

She placed her hand above the lamp shade and blew. The light went out. After a moment, the light came back on. Minno held up a thumb switch for Hailey to see.

"It's not magic. It's a thumb switch. Grampa likes to make you think he knows magic."

She then switched the lamp off again. In the darkness Minno's eyes turned silver, though Hailey, who had already turned away, never noticed. A square block of ashen moonlight fell into the room, painting their faces as they slept. Hailey's wore a smile.

Downstairs, Esri switched off the dim hanging bulb above the sink, after which, he began his slow walk to the closet-sized bedroom at the rear of the cottage. As he did, the old mare bucked in her corral, stomping about in a frenzied circle.

The plates in the cupboard behind him shook as if something monstrous stomped their way. With his back to the window in his bedroom, Esri never noticed the strange blue light pulsing above the trees in the neighboring forest. Nor because of his failing hearing, did he hear the distant, unnerving shrill that awakened the night.

As Esri settled into his sagging cot, a hummingbird whizzed in through his open window to hover beside his head.

Upstairs, Hailey slept soundly when the bed suddenly shook. A trembling hand clamped Minno's mouth, awakening her with a start.

"Big trouble. We must go," Esri said.

Seeing the terror in Esri's eyes, Minno knew to ask no questions and comply immediately. She stumbled out of bed, while Esri awakened Hailey on the other side.

"Dress quickly, we must leave," he said, his voice fraught with concern.

Hailey had no idea what was happening, but seeing her friend climbing into her clothes in a frantic way meant she must do the same. In a moment, Esri returned down the ladder while the girls tied their shoes.

Esri waited as they came down the ladder: First Hailey, then Minno. He led them directly to a rear window, where before exiting, he placed Minno's leather bag over her shoulder.

"Everything you need is in your bag," he said cryptically. Then he assisted each as they climbed out into the night.

Minno immediately noticed their corral gate had been trampled through and their mare was nowhere in sight.

"Grampa, what's going on?"

Before Esri could answer, yellow flames flashed over the cottage roof. The girls screamed as Esri led them into the field away from the house.

"What's happening?" Minno yelled.

Flames engulfed the cottage roof, lighting up the night sky.

"Where we going?" Minno asked, terrified now by what she saw.

"To the portal," Esri called back. He led the way, pulling the girls along as best he could.

"The portal. What portal? Grampa, what's happening?"

Esri refused to stop until the three were fully ensconced in the woods behind their cottage, which was now completely engulfed in flames. He sucked in deep breathes, using a tree trunk to steady himself. At his advanced age, running took every ounce of strength he could muster. Worry consumed his eyes.

"I don't understand. What about Hailey?"

"I'll see her safely home once you are through."

Esri wanted to resume moving. But Minno clamped his arm to hold him fast before her. Her terrified eyes begged for an explanation.

"Minno, when I said your parents had died in a car crash, I wasn't exactly being forthright," Esri blurted in a rush.

"You're saying my parents *aren't* dead?"

"Yes, exactly. They're alive, but they're in grave danger. You must rescue them."

"Me? How? What was that thing back there?"

"He sent an Arachnorock through. We have to get you to the portal before it closes."

The hummingbird from Esri's bedroom swooped in, hovering so they could see it in the light from Esri's flashlight.

"We must hurry."

Esri pushed deeper into the forest, playing his flashlight off the hummingbird leading the way. The girls followed, Hailey clinging to Minno.

"What portal? Arachnorock. My parents aren't dead."

"I know. There was so much I was supposed to tell you. But I thought we would have more time. We must hurry now."

With the hummingbird as their guide, the three wove through gnarly tree limbs, gravitating toward the blue light growing more intense with each stride. Minno could feel her heart racing with her feet. So many things swirled inside her head that she couldn't focus on any one of them. But at the forefront stood the fact that her parents were alive.

The trees at last opened to a clearing surrounding a jagged rock formation jutting up from the ground. At the center of the rock formation, a crevasse emitted the strange blue light that painted the trees, and their faces, as they approached. A sucking wind howled from within the opening, whose jagged split appeared wide enough for Minno to easily slip through.

Esri stopped them a few feet from the opening, positioning them to one side. He lowered himself to come face to face with Minno. His trembling hands took her shoulders.

"Antinarra is the key to finding your parents."

"The portal. Auntie Narra. Go back to my parents are alive," Minno insisted.

"I wish I had more time to explain. I should have told you. But I was afraid you were too young to understand. Remember, everything you need is in the bag. Never allow anyone to take it from you, and most importantly, tell no one where you came from."

"Yes, but . . ."

Tears came to Minno's eyes. She realized in that moment that she was about to leave her grandfather. She would be going alone on this journey. But at the same time, the thought of her parents actually being alive exhilarated her; the thought of leaving her grandfather behind terrified her.

"What if I can't do it?"

Esri took her face into his hands.

"Minno, you must believe in yourself as much as I believe in you."

Minno threw her arms around his neck, hugging him as tightly as she could. Against all sense, Esri had to pull her away. Hailey was straying too close to the opening.

"No!" Esri yelled over the loud rush, just as the howling wind sucked Hailey into the portal's blue light.

"What are we going to do?" Minno screamed.

"You must go now. Remember, Antinarra. No one must know where you came from," Esri said. He handed her the flashlight before easing her toward the blue light.

"How do we get back?" a frightened Minno pressed. Fear held her feet fast to the ground.

"Don't worry. Your parents will know. I will hold off the Arachnorock. Remember everything you've learned."

"Grampa, I haven't learned any ..."

At that moment Minno felt the air suck her into the opening. She looked back in time to see Esri turning toward the night as a giant clawed arm came swiping in to knock him from his feet.

"Grampa!" Minno screamed.

The swirling air swallowed her up into the darkness of an unending tunnel.

5

Minno rode the air currents as if she had been pulled onto a fantastic, wild luge ride. She screamed when she dipped, descending into pitch darkness. Hurtling downward at what felt like eighty-miles-an hour, she repositioned the flashlight on her chest until it pointed the beam in front of her. A distance ahead she glimpsed another body—Hailey she presumed—sailing along, rising and twisting also.

"I'm coming, Hailey," she yelled, though in the howling wind she was quite certain Hailey would never have heard her.

Minno extended the flashlight further, only to have it knocked from her grasp by something over her head. When she began to drop suddenly, the way a roller coaster plummets, she sucked in her breath and tucked her arms and head to her chest. There was nothing she could do but allow the force, as it were, to take her where it intended her to go. Despite the weightless sensation she experienced, she remained undaunted. This mysterious force that now held her suspended felt like cradling hands, enveloping her, and keeping her from harm.

Despite the breakneck speed and bone-jarring twisting and dropping, Minno felt no fear. The downward shaft seemed unending as she fell further into a lightless abyss.

Then she leveled off, seeing a faint yellow light that grew in the distance. Magically Minno slowed, as if some cosmic force were braking in anticipation of her arrival. She swooped to a soft landing inside a vaulted cavern, where shafts of vibrant sunlight pointed to a way out into full daylight.

She could see Hailey's footprints leading out of the cavern.

"Grandpa, no!" she called out on her knees. She wanted to lie down and cry. That thing back in Blue Lake had gotten him. Instead, she frantically wiped at her tears, but nothing she did could slow the rush from her eyes. For a few moments she sobbed, then she realized she was now alone, and she needed to find Hailey.

"Hailey! Where are you?" she called out. "Oh, wait," she corrected. Maybe yelling was a bad idea in this place.

In minutes, night had become day. It was near midnight in the place she left. Here it was clearly day. But what time exactly, she had no idea. And exactly where was here?

After brushing herself off, Minno wandered into the muted sunlight of a forest smothered by a tightly woven crown canopy. Only errant shafts of sunlight found their way to illuminate the cavern's opening. Tall sprawling ferns, standing taller than her, and strange inverted waist-high mushrooms grew everywhere she looked. The treetops towered easily eighty feet above the forest floor, with their trunks twice as thick as any trees she had ever encountered in California.

Minno checked her cell phone. **NO SIGNAL.**

Great.

"Hailey!" she called out, only half as loud as a full yell. She scanned the surrounding forest. No sign of her friend.

Then she spotted something moving ahead of her at least a hundred yards away. She couldn't be certain, but she hoped it was Hailey. Why hadn't Hailey just waited for her? Maybe Hailey didn't realize she had come through the portal right behind her. Hailey might think she's alone.

"Hailey, I'm here!"

Minno kicked into a run. As she gained on the silhouette in the trees, she became more confident it was her friend. But Hailey kept moving away from her toward a sunlit opening to their right. It appeared to be a forest clearing where sunlight fell through.

Minno closed as quickly as she could. She needed to catch up. She could see Hailey clearly now as her friend slowed near the clearing's fringe.

Then Hailey stopped.

Minno closed in. She wanted to call out, but she was so winded from running she couldn't breathe, let alone yell at the top of her voice.

Tree limbs snapped! The ground rumbled beneath her feet. Terror grabbed Minno as she watched Hailey stop in the clearing. Something huge and dark was lumbering through the trees toward her friend.

"Hailey!"

Minno reached the clearing's edge.

A huge, screaming man-like creature breached the clearing only twenty feet from them. As it did, a lanyard snared the creature's legs, toppling it face forward into trampled grass.

For a moment nothing moved, not the creature, not the girls.

Then the creature pulled his face up—it remained hidden behind soft mushy earth. Timid, fawn-like eyes stared at Hailey and Minno, who stared back in equal amazement, unable to speak, unable to force their feet to move.

The girls' eyes darted to the trees, where Nole, a man old enough to be their father, and wearing leather chest armor while brandishing a sword, leapt upon the fallen creature's back. He vaulted his shining blade skyward in triumph. Nole's rugged face remained smileless, but he had kind blue eyes. Not something one might expect to see from someone wielding a sword while standing over a huge forest creature. Sweat rolled down his cheeks.

"You've fought well, beast, but you have fallen. Accept your fate," Nole said.

Removing a steel reinforced leather band from a pouch, he placed it around the creature's neck. Afterward, he quickly attached a chain to the band.

During the entire process, the creature made no effort to oppose Nole, nor did he struggle once he hit the ground. Though clearly he stood three feet taller and seemed he must be stronger than the man upon his back.

"Trolls can be ill-tempered. You should stand back."

"Trolls? Yeah. We'll back up," Minno replied politely.

Hailey's unyielding look of disbelief begged a response from her friend. Yet Minno could find no words to explain what they were looking at, or for that matter, where they were.

As Minno and Hailey retreated, uncertain of what to expect next, Nole tugged the chain to bring the formidable troll to his feet.

"What are you two doing out here? You alone? Where is your handler?" Nole fired off in rapid succession.

"Our handler?" Minno queried. What possibly could that mean?

She shrugged in response to Hailey's confused expression. Hailey suddenly motioned for Minno to snap a photo of the scene. Her own outdated cell phone lacked one of those camera things on it. But Hailey hoped Minno's had one.

"Yeah, excellent idea," Minno said, withdrawing her phone from her pocket. She pointed it at Nole, who seemed perplexed by the device and the girls' actions.

Click!

Nole atop a troll now frozen inside her phone.

"Nobody back home is going to be believe this."

"You two should not be in troll territory without a handler. No matter. I shall see you safely to the fortress," Nole offered, sheathing his blade.

Nole tugged the chain further to bring the creature that shared many human characteristics, while also having some non-human characteristics, to its feet. The troll cleared away the mud to reveal a cherub face that appeared quite handsome as trolls go. He also stood at least eight feet tall, maybe closer to nine. Black matted hair covered his arms and torso, though his adolescent face had none. His eyes were exactly like Nole's, but his oversized ears flopped when he moved. His webbed feet had the requisite five toes, while his fingers had claws rather than fingernails, probably suitable for digging. He wore green leather breeks ending just below the knees and held secure around a barrel waist with a knotted rope.

As Nole tugged the chain, the girls skirted around the troll, giving it a wide berth. Despite the creature's docile look and demeanor, Minno thought it best they not venture too close.

With chain in one hand, Nole drank noisily from an animal-hide flask with the other, allowing red wine to dribble down his chin.

"Sir, we're terribly thirsty. Could you spare something to drink?"

Nole eyed them then set the flask at his side.

"Let's move out," he ordered as if commanding soldiers.

They walked for hours to reach the end of the dense forest that opened into a gently sloping valley with a footpath winding through it. The afternoon sun warmed them once they emerged from beneath the leafy crown canopy, and both girls relished leaving the chilly damp trees behind. Hunger pains rumbled through their stomachs. They wished at least for some water to drink.

"So, where do we get water around this place," Minno asked.

Nole ignored her question.

"How much further? We're really getting hungry from all this walking. When are we going to be there?" Minno asked, spacing each question a few seconds apart, in case Nole wanted to answer.

Hailey snagged Minno's wrist to stop her. Then she took up a stick to write in the dirt.

WHERE R WE?

"I don't know," Minno replied.

Using her foot, Hailey brushed the dirt like an eraser to write again.

WHERE WE GOIN?

"Don't know that either," Minno responded quickly.

Hailey wiped and wrote once more.

IT WAS NIGHT NOW ITS DAY

"Duh? I noticed that, too," Minno said, allowing unwanted anxiety to creep into her voice.

Nole kept walking during their exchange, moving further and further ahead of them. Minno wanted to resume their pace to catch up. But Hailey stepped on Minno's foot to hold her while she wrote again.

HOW WE GETTIN HOME?

Minno didn't answer. Rather, she pressed ahead to get back close to Nole. They would never be able to find their way back to the portal now. They had left the forest behind, and she could only hope they could locate her parents, who would help them find the portal when it came time to return home. Just the thought of home made Minno's heart drop. Her grandpa might be ... she refused to allow herself to even think of what might have happened to him.

In the passing hours of their journey Nole had said nothing. At times it seemed like he had forgotten they were even accompanying him. And at all times, the troll followed dutifully behind them, at chain's length, making no effort to resist his captor.

Their comfortable pace through the valley ended, replaced by an arduous craggy uphill climb using a rutted path on a sparsely covered hill. As they trudged, the path narrowed until it skirted a drop that grew steeper with each passing step. Hailey inched closer to Minno to avoid straying close to the edge. At times, the narrowing path forced the troll to slow and slide one foot in front of the other to maintain his footing.

Without warning, a spear-shaped crystal quartz rock jutted up from the ground, blocking their path and causing Hailey to stumble toward the cliff's edge.

She screamed—but her scream, of course, remained silent.

The rock ledge crumbled beneath her tenuous footing.

Hailey teetered, waving her arms wildly to find her balance. She was slipping over the edge!

The troll shot a hand out to snare Hailey's collar. He drew her back to safety not a moment too late.

Nole spun, unsheathed his sword, taking it to the troll's throat.

"Back, filthy troll. Unhand her."

In that moment, Hailey's eyes met the troll's. She saw in his kindness and desperation. She detected neither fear nor hatred. Hailey smiled as she mouthed her appreciation.

The troll released her, backing away from the sword. Hailey and Minno watched as the troll tried to smile, though his contorted face came out looking more scary than friendly.

"She can't talk," Minno offered to the troll.

"No talking to the troll," Nole scowled.

"Of course, I should've known that. What's wrong with me," Minno countered, her sudden sarcasm lost on the man. Minno was liking the troll hunter less and less as time went on.

Thirty minutes later they crested the hill only to face an equally steep descent to a woody valley below.

The raucous commotion of men fighting bounced off the trees in the midst of the woody valley. The Oogly brothers, Moogly, Doogly and Foogly, were in another of their frequent take-no-prisoners brawls. Though, this one was indeed worthy of the tumultuous scuffle that engaged the three.

Doogly, the oldest, and sporting the thickest mustache of the brothers, leapt over Foogly, who pulled himself to his knees, scrambling for the object that had instigated their latest altercation.

An unearthed egg horn lay in the dirt just beyond Foogly's outstretched fingers. Before Doogly could get it, Moogly kicked it away. Then she punched Doogly sharply in his ribs. His cry of agony shattered the surrounding quiet forest.

"Oh, no you don't!" Moogly shouted. She dove. Moogly sported a sparse mustache, she being the lone female of the three. Since females were poorly treated throughout the land, Moogly had decided she would become one of the Oogly brothers. All three wore faded green jackets helping them blend more effectively within the surrounding growth. None wore leather chest armor nor carried swords. The honor of wielding steel was one the Ooglys had yet to earn. Each had reached the age of thirty without advancing past the menial role of foot soldier.

But their unique talents earned them treatment far superior to any of the kingdom's soldiers.

"I seed it first. That makes it mine," Foogly grimaced. He shot his arm out full extension despite his agonizing pain.

"Says who?" Doogly sniped, jumping Moogly's back to knock her flat into soft earth.

"Suck dirt, you bugger eater!" he chimed.

"I'm gonna rip your arms from their sockets if you don't get off me," Moogly fired back, her words were muffled by her faceful of dirt.

Foogly used the opportunity to dive onto the precious egg horn and cover it with his body. This particular artifact was no larger than a man's fist, and it certainly contained no gold nor other precious metal. Yet the Oogly's were taking blood and punches in order to have it.

"I'm taking the egg horn. I need it more than either of you," Moogly said.

Suddenly the fighting stopped. The air became eerily silent. The Oogly brothers all froze in place. Like dogs, they sniffed in every direction. The egg horn no longer dominated their desire. Something else had usurped that.

"Troll!" Foogly chimed.

"See, I told you that egg horn is lucky," Doogly said, pointing a bitten and bleeding crooked finger.

Foogly scampered into the trees. With each stride, the Oogly brothers increased their speed until they reached full pelt. As they neared a rise, they fell to their knees, crawling the remaining twenty feet on their bellies to reach the crest.

On the rutted path below, snaking through the woody valley, Hailey lengthened her stride to get beside Minno, who had fallen further behind Nole. Hailey tugged Minno's sleeve to gain her attention, and using her face, she communicated her 'What's going on?' expression of shrugging shoulders with upraised hands.

"Wish I knew," Minno whispered back. Then she turned to Nole, who maintained his determined pace despite having children in tow.

"Excuse me, sir, but we really need to get to Auntie Narra. Could you tell us ..."

Nole stopped. He turned back to glare at Minno as if she were a nuisance circumstance had forced him to contend with. The four suddenly froze.

The Oogly brothers blocked their path.

Nole forgot what Minno had asked. He turned back to face the Ooglys, each clutching a spear, with crossbows and quarrels slung across their backs.

"Well, well, well. If it isn't Nole with a troll," Moogly said, eyeing him cautiously. Her brothers closed ranks beside her, just so Nole understood he would not be passing unchallenged.

Foogly laughed maniacally.

"Nole with a troll. Funny," he added when his laughing finally subsided.

Minno detected the contempt in their eyes for Nole, and their familiarity with each other certainly hinted a history between them.

"Hello, Nole. Nice troll," Doogly added, grinning stupidly.

Nole tightened a fist around his sword, the other on the chain. His jaw locked. His eyes narrowed. The chain rattled when the troll backed up a step in response to the advancing Oogly brothers.

Minno edged closer to Hailey, who eased next to Nole.

"The Oogly brothers, or is it the ugly brothers, how nice," Nole said calmly, his voice absent of sarcasm, or fear, for that matter.

"Oh, now that hurts," Moogly said.

The Ooglys all smiled at once, revealing their carious teeth as if they were somehow proud to display them. Foogly shifted his spear, reinforcing to Nole that they were dangerous and not to be cast off lightly.

"Specially coming from you, Nole," Doogly added.

"I always thought we was friends," Foogly offered.

For a lingering moment they stared at each other. No one blinked; no one moved. If Nole were intimidated by these Ooglys, he concealed it from both them and the girls.

Minno had no idea what to expect next. But in a flash she decided she would grab Hailey, and they'd break for the trees if Nole unsheathed his sword. Until then, she would hold her ground beside Nole, praying they could avoid getting caught up in this conflict.

"There's nothing for you here. Move along, Ooglys," Nole said. The words broke the tense silence hanging between them. They acted neither like enemies, nor like friends.

The Ooglys lowered their spears, but only a little.

"Looks like he got hisself a nine-footer," Foogly commented.

"Ha! No more than eight. Nole take down a nine-footer by hisself?" Moogly added.

"Maybe dese little girls helped. Did they help you, Nole?" Doogly pried with a raised suspicious brow.

The three brothers laughed a haughty, condescending laugh.

"Little girls? Excuse me," Minno forced in.

Moogly's menacing glare quickly quieted Minno.

That was a mistake. Minno realized she should avoid getting in the middle of their quarrel, whatever it might be.

The Ooglys closed in further, on Minno and Hailey, that is. They began sniffing them all over, causing the girls to tense up. But they remained rooted in the path.

"I'm thinking somebody could use an escort back to the fortress. Never know what beasts lurk in dese trees," Doogly offered, though the glint in his eye lacked sincerity in his offer.

"How considerate of you, Foogly. Now step aside," Nole answered.

"I'm Doogly. That's Foogly," Doogly shot back, gesturing to clarify who was who.

It wasn't exactly Nole's fault for the confusion. The Ooglys all looked alike, and to make it even more difficult to tell them apart, they all acted alike. Anyone might make the same mistake. Minno no longer even tried to keep their names straight. She just hoped they would get through this and never see the likes of the Ooglys again.

"I thought that was Moogly," Nole countered.

"I'm Moogly. Foogly's the ugly one," Moogly chimed in.

"Wouldn't wanna lose that eight-footer on the way to the fortress?" Foogly asked rhetorically.

"You mean that fortress?" Nole replied, pointing beyond the edge of the forest to a towering crystalline structure with multiple turrets and jutting spires not more than a mile distant. The sprawling fortress stood as an adjunct to the base of a mountain range. However, all plant life surrounding the structure lay dead, or withered and dying.

"Yeah, that one," Doogly said.

"I think we'll be fine." Nole inched his sword up in its scabbard. "Now step aside."

Nole tugged the troll's chain. The Oogly brothers reluctantly peeled back, allowing them through. Once the four passed, the Ooglys huddled briefly on the path before falling in to march a dozen paces behind the girls.

"Such a temper, Nole," Doogly said.

Foogly advanced closer to the girls, sniffing them again.

"You don't smell like you're from around here," he commented.

Minno ignored him, though having him close made her hair stand on end, while jolts of uneasiness coursed up her spine. She latched onto Hailey's arm and quickened their pace to get astride Nole.

At the core inside the fortress walls, the bustling market square fell silent as onlookers peeled backed for Nole and his troll. All eyes followed their every step. Then the girls entered the square, followed by the Oogly brothers. But their order changed. The Ooglys quickly advanced around the girls to come beside the troll.

Smiling big time, the Ooglys pointed to the troll as if it were their catch. Foogly even grabbed hold of the chain, which he vaulted, clearly implying ownership in their prize.

"It's a nine-footer, at least," he called out to any and all who would listen above the din of merchants who had resumed hawking their wares.

Doogly pointed to himself as if to imply he had brought the huge beast down. Cheers and applause echoed off the striated crystalline outer fortress walls as the group made their way to the keep.

When Nole abruptly stopped the troll before the towering doors of the fortress' keep, Doogly rammed into Foogly, who then rammed into Moogly. Two guards in hammered-steel armor receded to allow them entry, as anyone producing a beast for bounty gained an immediate audience with the high minister.

Inside the vaulted grand hall of the fortress keep, men in red robes clustered near the dais as throngs of peasants and soldiers crowded the expansive room. Blackbirds and sparrows, along with a smattering of white doves, fluttered about in the thirty-foot heights, soaring from crystalline arch to stone support as if vying for a view of the proceedings below.

Fluttering amongst the birds she recognized, Minno also spotted dozens upon dozens of huge insects with gyrating gossamer butterfly wings of varying colors. The harsh light, though, made it impossible to discern the body shapes of the insects, though she could tell they were certainly larger—and much different—than any she had seen back home.

All stopped. The red robes turned on Nole's entrance. Silence fell upon the room as the string threaded their way to the elevated dais.

The red-robed men withdrew to reveal a black-robed high minister, sitting upon his throne at the rear of the grand hall. Dirty, worn bandages covered both the high minister's eyes, or rather his eye sockets, since his eyeballs were in fact gone. Red gnarled scars—where dragon claws had torn the flesh from his face—revealed the story behind the high minister's grotesque disfigurement.

Suspended on the wall behind the high minister, a life-sized painting displayed the once-handsome man before his clash. His flowing black robe distinguished him easily from the sycophants that attended him on a regular basis. He offered no smile, no glimpse through his face into his soul or his demeanor.

Was this a kind man? Minno wondered while they made their way to the forward-most position before the dais in the vaulted hall. She could feel Hailey pressing against her from behind, her friend more frightened now than she had been when they first came upon the troll in the forest.

The high minister's face alone invoked trepidation in those that came before him.

"What have we here?" the high minister asked. His gruff voice modulated with an accent slightly French, though Minno had never heard it before. He delivered his words slowly, deliberately.

"A nine-footer," Moogly chimed.

Nole had to squeeze through the Ooglys, who each held the chain to bow deeply before the high minister.

"It is my catch, high minister, from the Forest of Perpetual Night."

The Ooglys turned to Nole, muscling their way beside him at the base of the dais.

"High Minister Craveaux, I present this beast for its authorized bounty," Nole continued despite the jostling caused by encroaching Ooglys.

Hailey dug her fingers into Minno's arm. Craveaux! Where were they? How could this be?

"Yeah, I caught that, too," Minno whispered back.

"I, or rather *we*, object, high minister," Moogly cast out in a strong confident voice.

Minno could feel the trouble brewing. She didn't know why; but she was certain something bad was about to transpire.

"This troll's bounty rightfully belongs to me," Nole insisted.

Moogly inched toward the dais, bowing slightly.

"My most highest high minister, forgive me, but Palladin law states only children *over* the age of sixteen may be used as bait for troll hunting," Moogly interjected as if she were an expert.

"What? No. These two, they were not bait. I came upon them wandering the forest. They had nothing to do ..." Nole pleaded.

"Theys don't look sixteen to me, your most high greatness ministerness," Doogly offered.

"High minister, we seed what we seed," Foogly reinforced.

"Yup, looked like bait to us," Moogly added.

Craveaux leaned forward in his high-backed crystalline chair, gesturing with a curl of his long-nailed index finger for Minno and Hailey to advance.

Neither girl moved.

"Little girls, stand before your high minister," the vaulted one commanded.

"First, we're not *little girls*. And second ..." Minno said.

"Si-lence!" Craveaux screamed, pounding the armrest.

Slam!

The entire room kissed the floor in unison, cringing and cowering to shield their heads with their arms ... all except for Minno, Hailey and the troll, who merely gazed around in amazement. Hailey, however, slipped behind Minno, just in case something bad might be forthcoming.

"Whoa," Minno said.

"Tell Craveaux your ages," the high minister commanded.

Once the tense moment dissipated, and Craveaux resumed a tone more civil, everyone returned to their feet. Yet no answer came.

"Craveaux speaks to you!" he said more like a father than an impatient ruler.

"Ah, Craveaux said not to talk. Now you're saying talk. Make up your mind," Minno offered, perhaps too stridently in her own defense.

Craveaux said nothing, but his face indicated he was not amused.

"All right. Thirteen. Almost fourteen. And for the record, we just stumbled into this guy in that forest of perpetual thing or other."

"You look different than most Palladins," Craveaux said, scrutinizing the girls, despite the absence of his eyes. His nose was pointing directly at them.

"Ha. That's funny, how would you ..." Minno replied.

Craveaux leaned forward toward Minno.

"How would Craveaux what?"

"Nothing," Minno answered.

"They smells different, too," Foogly added.

The high minister leaned back in his chair, placed a hand to his chin to deliberate over the matter brought before him. After a few silent moments, he lowered his hands to the armrests to signal he had reached a decision.

"Palladin law is clear. Using children under the age of sixteen to trap trolls is forbidden."

Disappointment took over Nole's face. He knew what came next. His heart sank into the pit of his stomach.

"Since we was holding the chain when we arrived, we, most highest high minister of all the land, master of the domains in which he so justly presides, hereby honorably do request the troll's bounty, as next in succession," Doogly said.

Craveaux considered the request, but only for a second.

"Since Craveaux cannot know if this troll hunter did so violate Palladin law by using these little girls as bait, Craveaux has no alternative but to decree the Oogly brothers shall have the troll's bounty."

Nole turned crestfallen. But he dutifully bowed, knowing he must accept the decision of the land's high minister. He refused to look over at Minno, but he did share a sidelong glance with the troll, whose face had turned ashen at the words, which was difficult to detect, since troll skin normally took on a pale birch-like hue.

"As my high minister commands," the troll hunter conceded.

"Remove them," Craveaux commanded, ending Nole's audience.

"Sorry," Minno offered Nole. She spoke barely above a whisper while soldiers tugged the troll away. She realized an apology meant nothing to him now. She had no idea what a troll fetched in this land, but certainly the troll hunter had lost it on account of them.

Thinking they, too, had been dismissed, Minno led Hailey behind Nole and the troll.

"Not you, little girls. You remain before Craveaux."

Not wanting to anger the high minister further, Minno dutifully led Hailey back. As she did, Hailey tugged her sleeve.

"Tell where you come from."

"The forest. Could you tell us where the bathrooms are?" Minno replied.

The robed men looked to one another confused.

"Do you need to take a bath?" Sickly, a robed seventy-year-old sycophant beside Craveaux asked.

"No, we need your restroom," Minno offered, hoping to clarify their pressing need.

"Oh, you need to take a rest," Sickly said, offering a puckered smile.

"Okay. Let's try this. We need to tinkle. You know what tinkle means, right?"

"Oh, you mean like the stars," Sickly pressed, perplexed by this ever-evolving request.

"Not twinkle. Tinkle. Where do ladies go when they have to, you know, go?"

"Oh. The consultory."

"Yes. We need to use your consultory."

At a pace consistent with his advanced age, Sickly led the girls from the dais down a side hall. On their exit Minno failed to notice that the eyes in the painting followed their every move.

The inviting aroma of roasted fowl wafted through the grand hall, as did the noise and the smoke from the hearths. Minno and Hailey found themselves seated at the table on the dais before throngs of soldiers and the peasant women serving them. Platters of meat and vegetables crossed before the girls on their way to soldiers' tables.

Famished from a day without food, Hailey stretched off her seat, hoping to snatch a piece of meat from a passing tray, but the serving woman swerved wide to keep Hailey from succeeding.

"When do *we* eat?" Minno at last asked of Sickly, who sat beside Hailey. Minno sat beside Craveaux.

"High Minister Craveaux feeds the men who protect him first."

"Great," Minno said, disappointed they would then be last to eat.

Hailey frowned. She lunged for a large purple pear on another passing tray. She missed again.

"That bag you carry, it is a gift for the high minister?" Sickly asked on the sly, making certain Craveaux wouldn't hear. The high minister busied himself waving to his men, while smiling his appreciation for the women who served them.

"No. My grandfather gave it to me," Minno snapped sharply, thinking it presumptuous they should provide a gift in the first place.

"Oh," was all Sickly replied.

Craveaux leaned close to Minno. His warmth, along with his odorous air, made her uncomfortable. So much so, that she leaned away, which brought a frown to his face.

"Where did you say you traveled from?" he asked casually.

"I didn't."

"Are you two from Homer valley? I thought I detected a bit of an accent," Craveaux pursued, feigning surprise, as if Homer valley meant something to them.

Minno shook her head. Finally, a platter of roasted game arrived at the dais. Minno lost the first leg to Hailey, who lunged for the food like a ravenous dog.

Minno took up what appeared to be another large, meaty chicken leg. She sniffed it—it didn't smell like chicken—before trying a small bite. Hailey, on the other hand, chomped into the meat, tearing it from the bone.

"This is excellent chicken," Minno offered, more to be polite to her host than to compliment the cuisine.

Craveaux laughed.

"It's seasoned squirrel."

A shiny ring of animal fat circled Hailey's lips as she looked over at the high minister.

"*Really?*" Minno responded, examining the leg. Just how big did the squirrel have to be to have a leg like this? "What's it seasoned with?"

"Why slugs, of course."

Hailey gagged, regurgitating the meat into her hand. She emptied her entire mouth before piling the chewed up mush neatly back onto her plate. Then she grabbed a roasted potato and slid the plate away.

After consuming his meal, Craveaux stretched back in his chair. When he did, Minno noticed a pulsating green gemstone suspended on a lavish gold-trimmed necklace around his neck. The stone's pulsations held her eyes. Initially she figured the light pulsed in sync with the high minister's heartbeat. How strange that seemed at the time.

"Did you not like the squirrel," Craveaux asked, turning as if he were looking at Hailey, which he couldn't be, since he had no eyes.

"She can't speak," Minno said.

"Craveaux thought maybe she didn't like the high minister."

"No, that's not it. Would be a good reason, though. She just doesn't speak."

"For how long have you been traveling?" Craveaux cleverly slipped in, hoping to catch Minno unguarded.

Nice try, but not good enough. Minno knew Craveaux would try extracting something useful from her. For the moment she felt safe in the notion that the high minister had no idea who they were and where they had come from.

"Oh, not long. A few days actually."

"And you traveled from?"

"Okay. If you gotta know, Blue Lake."

"Which one?"

"Which one what?"

"Which blue lake?"

"Huh? No. Not which blue lake, Blue Lake."

"No. Which blue lake? All lakes are blue."

"Duh? We learned that in third grade. It's Blue Lake."

Craveaux grew anxious. This little girl was toying with him. And becoming insolent. But her evasiveness elevated his suspicion. Perhaps he should learn more about these two little girls who claim to have come from the forest.

"Then tell the high minister which lake, that happens to be blue, you are from."

"Look. It's not which lake that is blue. It's Blue Lake."

"If it's blue lake, then it's a lake that happens to be blue!"

"Ya know what. Never mind," Minno stated, hoping Craveaux would allow his failed interrogation to end unfruitful.

With a snap of his fingers, Craveaux leaned away from Minno to summon Sickly to his ear. For a decrepit old man, Sickly surged out of his chair, shuffling over to his high minister without delay.

Minno casually shifted toward Craveaux despite his barnyard smell. She strained to listen, but the high minister spoke so softly only Sickly could hear.

"Find that troll hunter," Craveaux commanded.

Minno decided she'd show him. Want to keep secrets, do ya? Minno leaned to Hailey's ear.

"We shouldn't have come here."

Hailey offered a cross look. Somehow having food to eat, water to drink and a place to sleep seemed way better than roaming a creepy forest filled with trolls and who knew what else lurking about.

"It is late. You both must be tired from your journey from your lake that is blue. Craveaux will see you to your bedchamber for the night."

As they exited the grand hall, Hailey snatched what she thought to be a hand-sized dried apricot from a passing platter. It squirmed to escape her grasp.

"*Yuck!*"

She recoiled, releasing it to drop to the floor. Life rule number four: *If it moves, don't eat it.* Evidently that rule didn't apply here.

The high minister led them through a maze of corridors, up a winding staircase, then through another corridor maze to reach their bedchamber, as he called it. All the while, Minno pressed her memory to retain the number of turns, along with the number of corridors, just in case that knowledge became useful in the future.

Craveaux threw open the door with grand fanfare to a magnificent high-ceiling circular chamber. The spacious oval bed in the center of the room was large enough for a sleepover for six girls. Crimson embroidered drapery enveloped the rear half of the bed, matching the long narrow window drapes directly opposite the door. An oil painting of Craveaux in his high minister robe with two small children beside him oversaw the room from the wall above the door. He was smiling in the painting as he gazed upon the innocent faces. Minno, however, derived no warm and fuzzy feeling from viewing the work of art.

Two statues of Craveaux in armor holding a magnificent sword flanked the bed as if to stand watch for those who slumbered there. In the painting, as on the statues, Craveaux's face was unscarred.

"I hope this is suitable," Craveaux said.

"You bet," Minno replied, scanning the room while Hailey hopped onto the bed to check out huge feather pillows on a leopard-patterned blanket.

Hailey quickly abandoned the bed in favor of a fruit bowl filled with round purple fruit on a side table.

"There's Yassah fruit, should you get hungry," Craveaux offered.

Hailey snatched up a particularly plump one to bring it to her lips.

"Uh-oh," she heard a tiny voice murmur. It came from the fruit.

As Hailey rotated the orb, an orange glowing worm sucked itself into a hole. Grossed out, she returned the fruit to the bowl. It seemed there was no 'normal' food to be had anywhere in this place. If she could talk, she would beg for a hamburger or at least a peanut butter and jelly sandwich to satisfy her hunger.

"Their worms are in season. On the morrow, we shall meet again, and you'll tell Craveaux more about your lake that is blue."

Hailey returned to the bed.

Craveaux's attention shifted to Nole, who stood outside the chamber beside Sickly. Minno's eyes met the troll hunter's. She tried to read his face. His expression sought to convey something to her without words. But Craveaux came between them, severing their visual connection. Yet she believed Nole was trying to send her an unspoken message. If only she could understand what it meant.

"Craveaux bids you a good night now."

The high minister backed out, closing the door on his exit.

Minno shifted quickly to the door, waving an arm for Hailey to stop her jumping. She leaned in to the keyhole. While she listened, Hailey left the bed to exam a pair of silver neck bands sitting beside the fruit bowl. The bands were solid silver, large enough to fit around the neck, but no so large that they could slip over the head once clasped.

Outside the chamber, Nole bowed before Craveaux.

"I swear, high ..."

Craveaux raised a hand to quiet Nole mid sentence.

Minno heard a key enter the lock, then a bolt slid across, locking the girls in.

"Exactly where in the forest did you come upon those two?" Craveaux asked.

"Beyond the fall of the western ravine ... in woodland troll territory. Why do you lock them away?"

"You question Craveaux?"

Sickly cringed at the very utterance of the words.

"Leave now!" Craveaux commanded.

"Perhaps," Nole ventured, "you would grant me the girls for training. They might make excellent bait for trapping trolls ... when they are older, of course," Nole finished.

No response from the high minister meant it was time to leave. Nole bowed and departed, leaving Sickly to escort Craveaux back through the corridor maze and down the staircase.

Inside the bedchamber, Minno left the door to join Hailey, who had unclasped one of the silver bands and placed it around her neck.

"Hailey, leave that, don't," Minno said, reaching for her.

Before Minno could stop her, Hailey closed the band around her neck. When the two clasp ends came together, sizzling blue light arced, fusing the clasp into one solid metal ring.

"You need to take that off," Minno scolded, returning to the bed.

Hailey jumped onto the bed beside her, where she worked the clasp with both hands. The clasp held fast. Frustration took over. Hailey tugged furiously at the band. It held around her neck.

"Let me try," Minno offered, moving behind her friend to work the clasp. The silver band had locked around Hailey's neck. It refused to be undone. After a few minutes of fruitless effort, Minno abandoned her attempt. She left the bed to pace the floor.

Hailey's face turned troubled when she read the concern across Minno's brow.

"We're prisoners, not guests," she said, looking back at the painting. This man was not the gentle man depicted on the canvas.

What're we gonna do? Hailey asked by way of her hands and arms.

"Not waiting for the breakfast specials, that's for sure."

9

For the next fifteen minutes Minno circled the room like a caged lion. Her face wore a frown; she was thinking hard. Her heart pounded. Hailey watched from the bed until she herself became dizzy. Then Minno realized they had only one option. She leaned sideways out the tall narrow window, which turned out to be just wide enough to squeeze through.

Their 'so-called' bedchamber was situated near the peak of a forty-foot tower. The sheer drop ended abruptly at a jagged ridge, washed in white light from the gibbous moon. For a moment Minno's hopes deflated as she assessed their chances for success. Then she realized a window similar to theirs existed ten feet below them. Her heart surged into her throat while she considered their only way to that window.

Minutes later, a bedsheet rope dribbled out their window, extending below the window one floor down.

Minno sized the distance again before pulling her head back in.

"We can do this," she coached Hailey, who stuck her head out for a quick glance. When she came back in, she vehemently shook her head in opposition to Minno's plan.

"You just lower yourself a little at a time, like they make us do in gym class. When you reach the window, swing inside. Just trust me," Minno reassured her.

Hailey stared back with incredulous eyes. Life rule number three: Never trust someone who says 'just trust me.'

"We can do this. I'll go first. Once I'm inside, you follow. I'll help you get inside. Can you do this?"

Hailey nodded she could. But her eyes were clouded by doubt. She shook her head no. Afterward, she crossed her legs like she had to use the bathroom.

"I know you're scared. So am I. But if we stay, Craveaux's going to keep us locked up here. I need to find my parents."

Hailey nodded in the affirmative.

They shared a hug before Minno wiggled her way through the opening, clutching the makeshift rope.

Minno knew if she dared look down, her entire insides would surge into her throat. She lowered her body a little at a time, using her feet to feel for the upcoming window. At last, her feet dangled in the air and in through the window. She lowered herself until she could transfer her hands from the rope to the window ledge. From there, she crawled inside and began to breathe again.

Moments later a terrified Hailey descended exactly as Minno had. When she reached the window, Minno clutched her waist to swing her safely inside. Both girls expelled huge sighs of relief. They were free, at least for the moment.

"We'll be long gone by the time Craveaux finds out," Minno reassured her friend. They crept to the door, grateful the room was unoccupied.

In silence, they navigated the smoky sallow corridor maze without error, dashing down the tower's spiral staircase until they reached the bottom, where they exited into a torch-lit vaulted hallway. Both girls hugged the crystalline stone wall, advancing while tuned for the slightest sound. It seemed the entire fortress slept, since no sounds rose to frighten them.

They reached their first crossing corridor. Minno paused, her plan quickly souring. She couldn't recall which direction led out of the fortress. They had earlier made so many turns to reach the bedchamber that now she became confused about which way would get them free of this place. Indecisive moments passed. Hailey pestered Minno to make up her mind.

"How would I know which way?"

Hailey pointed one way, Minno the other. Minno decided to defer to Hailey, hoping her friend's instincts were better than hers in this situation.

Minno felt the burden of responsibility bearing down on her for her new friend's safety. If she chose incorrectly, they might end up right back before Craveaux. Then it'd be back to their tower prison with no way of escaping this time.

As they progressed down the corridor, Minno found herself accelerating, which forced Hailey to break into a jog to keep up with her.

Voices!

And they grew louder with each passing second. Minno's heart raced as she scrambled to figure out what to do next.

She spied a door ahead on their left. They were out of options. The voices sounded just paces away now. Minno grabbed Hailey, pulling her in through the unlocked door. Then she closed it as soundlessly as possible.

They were safe for now—they hoped.

The room appeared to be some kind of power chamber, bathed in a greenish glow. At the core of the twenty-foot vaulted space, a huge egg-shaped rock spun while suspended without attachments over a crystal stone altar. An array of hoses and crude pipes ran along the side wall of the room then wound around the stone's upper half.

Just inside, a pair of ten-foot statues of Craveaux flanked the doors.

The spinning stone emitted the green glow flooding the windowless chamber. Though it spun quite rapidly, the room remained deathly silent, allowing the growing voices to penetrate the door and alert the girls to their advancing danger.

Minno helped Hailey onto a large pipe, which allowed them to retreat to the far side of the chamber beyond the stone's glow. As soon as they reached the darkness, the chamber door opened.

Craveaux entered with Sickly, followed by two red-robed ministers. They stopped before the spinning stone, and while standing there, Craveaux exposed his necklace. The green stone Minno had observed during dinner seemed very dim now.

"More power," Craveaux snapped between clenched teeth.

Sickly responded by advancing upon the spinning stone, where he took hold of a large oaken lever beside the altar. With agonizing groans, he pulled with all his strength. But the lever barely budged. Craveaux's necklace remained dim.

"Put your back into it, Sickly," Craveaux commanded, angrier now.

The two other ministers scurried to assist. Through all three's backbreaking efforts, the lever moved, causing Craveaux's necklace to brighten. The stone began to hum.

In the darkness, the girls removed their hand hold on the pipe to cover their ears, causing them to falter. Both almost fell, but the girls latched onto each other at the last second to remain on top of the pipe.

"High minister, opening the portal has consumed enormous power," Sickly whined. "We must close it …."

"No!"

Suddenly, crystal rocks jutted up through the floor. Craveaux's power was expanding. The crystals would shield him from the magic of the creatures he sought to destroy.

"Yes, more, you worthless whiny weasels," Craveaux commanded.

The high minister turned to an outer wall. He spread his arms full length while mumbling words only he understood. A wavering window appeared, revealing the moonlit landscape beyond the fortress.

Through the magic window Craveaux watched crystalline shapes erupt from the silver-painted landscape. They formed low walls that expanded the reach of the high minister's fortress. As long as he remained surrounded by the powerful Beuteline crystals, no creature in Ambrosia could vanquish him. The Beuteline provided him with a potent magic all other creatures feared. And as long as they feared Craveaux, he could advance his plan.

"Yes! Much better," the high minister chimed, allowing the men to release the lever and return to their leader.

Beyond the fortress, the giant crystals slowed their spread along the ground. After another moment they stopped all together.

"What! They stopped!" Craveaux grumbled.

"We are full throttle. It is all we have," Sickly offered.

The words, along with the lack of progress outside, clearly angered the high minister. Craveaux dismissed his magic window with a sharp wave, returning the chamber to the stone's green glow. Then he returned his attention to the huge egg stone.

"Order the soldiers to round up all creatures immediately. Double the bounties, if necessary."

"All creatures? Surely this will raise suspicions," Sickly risked.

"This is not a request. Craveaux needs their magic quickly."

Sickly, realizing his err, bowed, then he took a slap from Craveaux.

"Yes, high minister, as you wish."

Sickly and the sycophants retreated to the door. But Craveaux remained behind. He had become uneasy. Something crawled under his skin. He peered into the darkness beyond the glowing stone. Something was out there, he could sense it. But he couldn't discern exactly what kept tugging insistently at his mind.

In response, Minno drew Hailey further from the huge rock.

"Follow me," she whispered weakly, frightened Craveaux might detect their presence. The urge to get as much distance between them and the high minister as possible overwhelmed her.

Inching along like caterpillars, they traversed the pipe until they reached a pipe tunnel cut into the chamber's wall. They squirmed their way into the pipe tunnel, swallowed up by the total darkness.

As the girls slithered along a curve in the pipe, a sallow flickering light appeared in the distance. Then a pair of huge red eyes bore down on them.

Hailey stopped, tried to scream—but her scream remained silent.

"Why you sto ..." Minno whispered harshly.

Then she saw the glowing eyes. And the glistening teeth. She opened her mouth to scream. Hailey clamped a hand over her mouth to keep her silent.

A huge gray rat behind the eyes screamed! Well more like a shrill squeak that lasted no more than a second.

Unmoving, both girls stared with wild disbelief. The rodent stood easily two feet tall. Its spiked teeth were visible in the darkness. For a moment Minno thought they were both about to be devoured.

The moment seemed endless. Then the rat turned tail and scurried away into the darkness of a side tunnel. Minno started to breathe again. That was close. She had no idea what she would have done if the rat chose to attack.

The girls moved in unison along the pipe watching the light grow brighter. They approached a lighted room emitting whimpering sounds.

Then came singing. Not just singing—off-key, operatic bellowing from a gruff, forceful voice.

The pipe tunnel opened onto a chamber bathed in smoky torchlight. Peering in from above, Minno spied a soldier a few feet below wearing elbow-length rubber gloves, a full-length leather apron and crude goggles on his forehead.

"So-fa Lu-cia, a-la du Sancti, brav-o Craveaux, our hero almighty," the soldier boisterously belted out.

Then Minno gazed beyond the soldier.

She gasped in horror.

The troll struggled against leather straps binding him to a long table. Hoses punctured his neck and his right arm. He whimpered every few seconds. There was no mistaking the terror in those timid fawn-like eyes. A painting of the Craveaux with scars and bandages stared down on him, so all who faced this room knew well who was their true master.

"Please, don't. I want my mommy!" the troll cried to no avail.

The soldier lowered his goggles, preparing for a troll-flesh explosion.

"Stop being a baby. It's the price you pay ... you're a troll," the soldier said.

"Please. N-o-o-o-o-o."

"Bel-lo long fel-low, Craveaux di solo," the soldier sang out.

He checked a small bucket near some kind of crude machine connected to the hoses. Another pipe left the machine, joining the main pipe holding the girls.

The soldier threw out his arm in dramatic fashion as his voice reached a vibrating crescendo.

Blam!

Minno crashed down upon the soldier, slamming his head into the table. He wobbled back up.

"Mommy!" he uttered, dazed.

Whack!

Hailey crashed down upon him next. The soldier sputtered under faltering knees then kissed the floor.

The girls slapped each other a high-five.

"Let's go!" Minno said.

But she stopped before reaching the door. Hailey stood without moving, staring at the terrified troll. She motioned toward the troll's terrified face.

"Please help me," the troll said barely above a whisper.

"You're not a scary monster, are you?" Minno asked.

The troll shook his head. Hailey smiled, offering a little wave.

"Can you help us get out of here?"

"Yes," the troll replied simply.

"We undo these straps, you won't eat us?"

Shock took over the troll's face.

"Eat you? That's disgusting. Do I look like a dragon to you?"

Minno looked to Hailey for approval. Hailey looked at the troll, helpless and sad. Hailey shot her thumbs up. While Minno released the troll's arms, Hailey unstrapped his feet.

"These people aren't very nice," Minno offered.

"I could have told you that."

"Do trolls have names?"

"I'm Gutty."

"I'm Minno. She's my friend Hailey."

Gutty wasted no time ripping the hoses from his arm and neck before jumping off the table. The three quickly headed for the door. But Gutty still couldn't fully trust the girls. They suddenly appeared out of nowhere to save him. How could that be?

Gutty assumed the lead, acting as if he knew exactly where he was going. Relief washed over Minno. She no longer had to figure out how to escape this terrible place. Or so she thought.

"Freeing me puts you in grave danger," Gutty said. He kept his eyes on the corridor ahead of them. All remained quiet, so he believed their escape had so far gone undetected. If only their luck could hold until they reached the doors leading to freedom.

"Yeah, somehow I think we were in full-on danger long before this," Minno said.

Gutty hesitated as they neared a crossing corridor in the fortress' underground maze. Hailey smiled at him when he looked back over his shoulder to make sure the girls were still behind him.

"This way," he said, indicating with his hairy arm that they take the corridor on their right, which in turn led into a tall and wide tunnel with torchlights every twenty paces.

Gutty removed a torch before venturing forth to illuminate an open expanse ahead of them. As they moved stealthily along, vicious screeching and thunderous flapping arose from behind two fifty-foot timber doors, with eye-level grated windows and a huge lock and chains securing them closed.

Hailey clung to Minno, who clung to Gutty, as they scurried past the doors and the giant iron lock.

"That's gonna wake 'em. Soldiers coming soon. We need to run!" he said.

Gutty hastened them out of the open expanse and into a vaulted chamber with a series of tunnels funneling into it.

"Wait ..." Gutty paused with uncertainty. "That way leads ..."

"You said you could get us out!" Minno snapped back, letting anger temper her voice. Her confidence in the troll was fast fading. She could only wonder how much time they had before someone discovered their escape and sent soldiers after them.

"I'm sorry," Gutty offered, his voice cracking.

"You're sorry? *You're sorry!*" was all Minno could get out before footsteps pounded into her ears.

"The troll is free!" a gruff voice shouted from a distance.

"We must run now," Gutty said.

They bolted from the chamber into the nearest tunnel, all hoping and praying it would lead them to an exit from the fortress.

Three tunnels away, and sniffing like bloodhounds, the Oogly brothers worked their way along, crossbows in hand. At a cross corridor, Moogly checked one direction, Foogly sniffed down the opposite.

"Nothing," Moogly reported.

"No way we're losing that bounty," Doogly grumbled.

"This way!" Foogly shouted from deep within another corridor.

Working their way as quickly as possible through the tunnel, Gutty used his massive hulk as best as possible to shield the girls when a crossbow quarrel zipped by over their heads.

Minno screamed!

"I hope we're almost there," Gutty cried out. He overtook the girls, pointing ahead. "This way!"

Gutty turned into another tunnel. He stopped dead in his tracks. The girls slammed into him from behind, spilling to the floor.

"Yuck, troll butt," Minno said, scrambling back to her feet while helping Hailey up.

Gutty stood face-to-face with Nole.

"Gutty, you're free!" Nole chimed with a rush of elation and relief.

"No thanks to you. What happened to I rescue you right after we get the bounty?" Gutty said.

"What? I was on my way ... honest."

Minno peered out from behind Gutty.

"You!" Nole said.

Hailey waved.

"What are they doing here?"

"No time. Soldiers coming. We gotta get out of here," Gutty added. They forged ahead in the tunnel. But now Gutty allowed Nole to assume the lead, who took them to a winding staircase that rose to ground level.

As the four raced up the stairs as fast as they could, soldiers stumbled over themselves to climb the stairs behind them. At the rear of the fallen mass of swords and armor, the Ooglys crawled over bodies to grab the lead on the chase.

Reaching ground level, Gutty and the girls followed Nole down the corridor, which was now awakening with the first weak rays of morning seeping in through high windows. The window openings, perched fifteen feet above the floor, were too high to allow them an escape.

When they chanced to glance over their shoulders, soldiers filled in at the end of the corridor with swords drawn. The Ooglys squirmed through to get to the front of the pack.

Nole stopped at a door at the end of the corridor.

It was locked! They were out of places to run.

"Move away," Gutty ordered, casting Nole aside.

Then the huge troll crashed into the door. Nole spun around, leveling his sword with the intent of fending off the soldiers and the Ooglys for as long as possible.

The Ooglys only chuckled as they advanced down the corridor in a casual way. The girls, the troll and the troll hunter were indeed trapped.

"Nowhere to go," Moogly commented, laughing.

"Hit it again!" Nole yelled as he backed closer to the girls.

This fight the four of them had no chance of winning.

Gutty crashed the door again—splitting it in two.

It opened!

The four spilled out the doorway, only to be hit with brisk morning air.

"Oh, great!" Minno cried out as they tumbled into the rushing river below.

10

Crossbow quarrels stabbed the water. The Oogly brothers crammed the doorway all firing at once. But all the brothers could do was hope they hit something.

A hundred feet downstream, Gutty bobbed to the surface, searching frantically. The girls were nowhere in sight. He tried swimming back, but the current pulled him along, making it impossible to change direction. He sucked in a mouthful of river water for his efforts.

Then Minno buoyed to the surface, thrashing wildly, gasping for air. She stretched her arms full length for anything to latch onto before going under again.

Gutty reached for her—he was too late! Minno slipped back beneath the surface. He twisted again. Out the corner of his eye he saw Hailey flailing between white water swells.

Gutty lunged. He snared her! Pulling Hailey against the current, he moved her onto his back.

"Hold on tight. I got you," Gutty yelled back.

Oh, no! Rapids! The white water swept them up, heading for waves rolling over submerged rocks.

Minno breached the surface again, held afloat this time by her inflated bag, which allowed Gutty to take her arm when the current brought them within reach of one another.

"Hurry, on my back," he commanded.

Minno thrashed using wildly uncoordinated strokes to keep hold of his arm.

"Hang on, Hailey!" Minno yelled, hoping to reassure her. From the terror in Hailey's eyes, Minno knew mere words were ineffective.

The three hit a waterfall. But as they spilled over, Gutty clamped onto a jutting rock ledge. As they dangled in the cascading water, Nole came splashing by, kicking with all his might to avoid the precipice.

"Hey!" was all he could get out before slipping over the fall. He stretched his arm out, but he fell short of reaching the troll.

Minno's grip on Gutty's arm hair faltered.

Gutty lurched, trying to tighten on Minno.

"I'm losing it ..." he said. His grasp on the rock ledge slipped. It released!

All three cannonballed into the pool below.

They uncurled while submerged beneath the churning water. Luckily, the pool was deep enough that none hit bottom, including Gutty. Despite the murk beneath the surface, Gutty could make out fish swarming in their wake, with more and more joining in.

"Out of the water!" Gutty cried out, hitting the surface, hardly able to speak while gasping to breathe.

The huge troll panic-paddled to the shore, lifting the girls onto the bank before dragging himself out and collapsing. He had no sooner crawled out when Nole washed up, flailing like mad to exit the water.

Lying in dirt near the edge of the undergrowth, and a safe distance from water's edge, Gutty turned to his side. A crossbow quarrel protruded from beneath his arm.

"You're hurt," Minno said.

Gutty yelped from Nole's clumsy effort to extricate the quarrel.

"Stay with him," Minno ordered, positioning Hailey to face her, so she could be certain Hailey understood her request. Hailey's gaze had turned vacant. Minno couldn't be certain her friend could process what she had just instructed her to do.

"Don't let them get me," Gutty moaned, swiping at the dirt as if to mound it between him and the shoreline.

After Minno disappeared into the greenery, Gutty used his good arm to crawl further from the water. Hailey tried to help him—but it was like pushing a mountain. For all her effort, she came up short in budging the huge troll.

Nole in the meantime became preoccupied.

"They're coming for us," Gutty moaned frantic.

"It's all right. We're safe now," Nole said, searching near the shore.

"No, we're not."

Minno returned carrying a handful of broad brown leaves with red veins, which she applied to Gutty's wound while Nole busily groped about near the water.

"I lost my sword," he muttered with insurmountable despair.

Hailey, meanwhile, gravitated toward the riverbank, fascinated by the gathering swarm of fish. A few feet from her, a long-whiskered catfish suddenly leapt upon the bank, where it flopped about frantically. However, it kept its bulging eyes fixed on Hailey.

"Help me. I've fallen and can't get up," it said with a gruff Spanish accent.

The talking fish snared Hailey's full attention. While she approached it, a grimacing Gutty worked his way to his knees with Nole's help.

"Some plan you had," Gutty said, gritting from the pain in his side.

"How could I know?" Nole started.

"I can't breathe. Oh, what a cruel world," the catfish moaned, drawing Hailey closer.

All the while, just beneath the water's surface, schools of fish formed into a small army preparing to attack.

"Help him. For Soma's sake, somebody help him!" could be heard in Spanish accents from bubbles popping at the surface.

"Uh ... Hailey. Hailey, don't!" Minno warned. She sensed the growing threat posed by the sudden mass of fish all focused around the point where the catfish flopped.

Disregarding Minno's warning, Hailey reached for the flopping catfish with every intention of saving it from certain death.

"No!" Nole yelled. He suddenly realized the fishes' strategy.

In the next moment, the fish leapt en mass, exposing their jagged teeth with a lot of yelling and screaming as they belly-flopped onto the shore! Large bulging fish eyes watched them.

"Get them, get them! Ha, ha! Lunch!" rang out.

Fortunate for the four on shore, the fish were far less mobile on land than they were in their native water.

"Move to their flanks," a shimmering green sunfish ordered as the other fish hit the bank, where they formed up into fighting units. The sunfish seemed in command, since they moved in response to his order.

But the fish mass moved away from the girls instead of toward them.

"No, you idyuts, their flanks! Surround them!" the sunfish commander yelled through gritted little teeth.

Minno reached Hailey just in time. She tossed her bag out. Hailey latched onto the strap. Minno yanked her back and out of the way of chomping little fish jaws.

"Run!" Gutty yelled, hobbling toward the undergrowth.

The fish scrambled toward them, using their fins like feet.

"Get back here and fight, you stinking cowards!" the sunfish commander yelled.

Nole remained behind, facing the hundred angry fish. Snapping a tree branch off a nearby pine, he swatted the attacking fish, rolling them backward long enough to allow the girls to move ahead of him. Before the fish could successfully mount their full scale attack, the four breached the underbrush and disappeared.

11

The warm afternoon sun in a cloudless sky dried them quickly. They walked along a rutted path that wound out of the forest and into a sprawling open valley. Nole and Gutty led, with the girls trailing a short distance behind. Though Minno had no idea where they were heading, it seemed Nole was in a hurry to get there.

"Can you take us to Auntie Narra?" she asked when it seemed they might just be wandering aimlessly.

"Not now, kid," Nole responded by rote.

"What happened to we collect the bounty, you free me so we can escape the fortress by nightfall?" Gutty said.

He kicked up dust clouds as he walked, which forced Minno and Hailey to shift to the side of the path. Growing impatient with Nole's lack of attention, the girls hurried ahead of the two to take the lead, since it seemed there were no alternate paths to use.

"And what was with attacking me in the forest?"

"When we ran into these two, I figured their handlers were close by. I had to improvise. I figured frightening you would sell it to them. Trust no one, remember."

"Can you at least tell me which is the way to Auntie Nar..." Minno stopped mid sentence.

Gutty was no longer the nine-foot troll they had encountered in the forest. With each step he shrank until he stood no taller than Nole. As a matter of fact, he became slightly shorter than Nole at the moment.

"How come you're?" Minno asked, astounded by the transformation.

"Oh, yeah, I get big when I get scared."

"Bigger the troll, higher the bounty, kid," Nole added.

The troll hunter looked around confused.

"Look, you two just cost us ..." Nole snapped at Minno, leveling a paternal finger in her face.

"They saved me, no thanks to you," Gutty said.

"Fine. What is it you want again, kid?" Nole interjected.

"To go to Auntie Narra. How far is it?" Minno replied.

"How should I know? Do I look like a traveler to you? We need to go," Nole said, directing his last statement to Gutty.

Gutty suddenly stopped. The ground rumbled. Crystal rock spears burst out in a jagged formation on the path.

"He's stealing more magic, growing more powerful. And what's with pulling your sword on me on the way to the fortress? You know I don't like that," Gutty said.

"You were starting to shrink. That would have blown everything. I had to scare you in order to sell it. We couldn't risk anyone tipping Craveaux off to our plan. They would have smelled us out if we didn't look real."

The girls stopped dead in their tracks.

"Hey! You going to help us or what?" Minno yelled.

Minno decided they were going no further unless their next steps helped them get closer to where they needed to go. And that was Antinarra.

"Yes," Gutty said at the exact same moment Nole said, "No!"

"Craveaux would have drained me and left me to die if these two hadn't come along when they did. For that, I will see them safely to Antinarra," Gutty continued, despite Nole's cross look.

"I told you. I was on my way to rescue you when you ran into me." Gutty shot Nole a mean face in response to his words.

"Do you even know where Auntie Narra is?" Minno asked.

"Well, no. But I have many cousins. One of them will know," Gutty explained.

"I got a bad feeling about this," Nole muttered as he scanned their wake. The Oogly brothers would likely be coming after their bounty. There was very little chance they intended give that up without a fight.

Gutty whistled. Within seconds three vibrant green hummingbirds descended out of the sky to hover near his head. But these hummingbirds were three times larger than any hummingbird Minno had seen at home.

"To Jaswor and Ismar and Levian. I must get to Antinarra. I am in the valley ..." Gutty said then paused. He scanned the rolling carpet of variegated flowers nearby. "The Valley of the Flowers beyond the Forest of Perpetual Night. Can you help?"

The hummingbirds took to the wind, each zooming off in a different direction.

"What was that?" Minno asked, amazed.

"Messengers. Don't you use them where you come from? Hopefully, one of them will return with directions."

"No, we use cell phones," Minno replied.

"That's really nice, kid," Nole said without looking back at her.

While they spoke, Hailey wandered off into the thick of the flower field. The wonderful fragrance of lavender and saffron bathed her. When she absently strummed a blue-petaled flower, the blossom hummed a note. She strummed another. This one, with white petals trimmed in crimson, produced a higher-pitched note.

Upon hearing the music, Minno left Gutty and Nole to venture into the flower field with her friend. Together they strummed a bevy of yellow and orange flowers, which resulted in a sonorous melody of violin music.

"This is way cool," Minno chimed, hardly containing her excitement.

Before long she and Hailey figured out the staff of notes and began stringing the different color flowers together into a song.

"It is very warm. Not cool. If it were cool, we would be shivering. I don't like the cool," Gutty offered.

"Hey, I think we should just go," Nole interrupted, growing more ill-at-ease the longer they remained in one place. His eyes roved from where they had come from to where they would go if they stayed on the path.

Minno strummed her song, stringing a dozen notes together in perfect harmony. Hailey followed with a complementing melody, as if they were dueling. She mouthed each note as if she were producing it herself. How sad that flowers in this place could produce something Hailey couldn't.

Gutty was taken watching Hailey's newfound happiness. The joy in her eyes at that moment convinced him he must see these two safely to Antinarra. *A kindness paid must be repaid in kind*, was the unwritten law for all creatures in this land. Now he must deliver on it, even if they were Palladins.

"No, it's like cool cool," Minno offered by way of explanation.

"Oh ... I see. That's nice," Gutty responded like an indulgent parent appeasing a child.

But an idea sprang into Gutty's head. It would be brilliant, if it worked. Careful so that neither girl saw his action, he palmed a vibrant blue blossom to tuck away out of sight.

"I think we should leave the flowers and get moving," Nole said with more than a little insistence in his voice.

But the music intoxicated the girls. Every time they tried to stop, the flowers called them back by fluttering in the breeze.

"This must be some kind of special magic. I've never heard flowers make music," Minno said.

Hailey and Minno played faster, racing from flower to flower to harmonize together.

By this time, even Gutty began to grow nervous. Something was wrong, yet he couldn't quite figure out what. A sinking feeling settled into the pit of his gut.

"You should stop now. We should get moving. Enough cool cool," he said.

But Minno refused. Nole took her hands to pull her back to the path.

"Just one more minute. Please!" she begged while squirming to free her hands so she could return to the flowers.

"Stop! You hear something?" Gutty suddenly burst out. He began growing again, his head rising above Nole's.

Minno realized what Gutty had heard.

"No .... Wait, a humming noise," Minno uttered.

"This isn't good," Nole said, scanning off to the cleft at the edge of the distant valley. A dark cloud rose into the otherwise clear sky. The cloud turned into a swarm of giant bees darkening the landscape.

"This is very bad," Gutty said. He returned to his nine-foot height. Instinctively, he brought Hailey under his arm to protect her.

"Oh, really?" Nole offered.

"What are we going to do?" Minno asked with panic-laced words.

"We can't outrun them," Gutty said.

"Back to the river!" Minno said. She started back the way they came. After a few paces, Nole snared her arm.

"The fish, remember," he warned.

"I will protect you," Gutty said to Hailey, bringing her tighter under his arm.

"Yeah, that's not going to work, Gutty. We need a better plan and fast," Nole said.

Nole took one step before crumbling to the ground, and there he began snoring.

"Oh, no, not now!" Gutty muttered.

"You've got to be kidding. He's sleeping? What's he doing?"

"Craveaux's spell. Cross him—he makes you pay. I told him not to do it; he did it anyway. He said we'd get even by stealing the bounty."

More symbolic than protective, Gutty placed himself between the girls and the bee cloud. He knew it was futile, but he had no other ideas to save them from the approaching menace. The giant swarm's buzzing grew more terrifying. The girls could now see the distinctive shapes of the individual bees in the swarm. They were that close, and each bee stretched the length of Minno's arm from their heads to their curved stingers. They could never outrun the buzzing creatures coming at them.

Reflexively Minno's hand tightened on her bag strap.

"Everything I need is in my bag," she muttered to herself, recalling what her grandpa had instructed just before they fled the cottage.

Minno opened the bag.

Sheer panic gripped her throat.

"There's nothing in here!" she called out, fighting back the tears that usually precede total collapse. But this was no time for crying. She had to think of something and think of it fast.

She shoved her hand into the bag, searching, only to discover she could extend her entire arm in. She yanked it out quickly. With eyes wide in amazement, she looked at Hailey.

Hailey's eyes followed suit with her 'what the ...' expression.

Minno jabbed her arm in again, then she dunked her entire head in.

"It's huge in here!" echoed out of the bag.

Another minute and the swarm would be on top of them.

Minno placed the bag on the path. There she opened the mouth as wide as possible.

"Everybody, in the bag!" she commanded.

Hailey and Gutty just stared at her. Neither could fathom what they had just heard. That was totally impossible, and they knew it. Minno was crumbling under the stress.

"You hit your head when we fell, that is it, isn't it? We need to run," Gutty said.

Hailey started back the way they came, attempting to drag Gutty along. But Minno stopped them.

"I know how this sounds. You have to trust me, or we're gonna get overrun by the bees."

Minno went first. She stepped into the bag and disappeared. Gutty set Hailey into the bag—and she disappeared. As the leading edge of the swarm of vicious bees reached the core of the flower field, Gutty scooped Nole up and they disappeared into the bag.

The flap came over the mouth of the bag to close it barely a moment before the bees pounced.

Inside the leather bag, Minno clutched Hailey while Gutty stood at his full height. Nole snored peacefully while curled to the side, still sound asleep.

"How can this be?" Gutty asked.

"I can't explain it. Just hold the flap closed."

At the same time Gutty reached the flap, a giant bee pried its head through. It bared canine incisors, barking like a vicious pit bull. The girls screamed! Gutty punched the head back out—another bee leaned halfway in, braying wildly. Gutty grabbed that bee's neck to shove it back out.

"Help me!" Gutty called back, but he realized the girls were too small to reach the opening, and the bee heads were too large for them to fight off. Gutty forced two more giant bee heads out as their frothing drool ran down his arms before sealing the flap.

Safe at last!

The huge troll settled beside the girls while holding the flap tight. Like popcorn popping, the giant bees pummelled the bag, trying to find some way to get inside.

"How long does he stay like that?" Minno asked, indicating Nole in the corner.

"I never know."

"We'll be safe as long as you keep the flap closed," Minno added.

"They will tire soon. Then they will leave," Gutty offered when he saw the terror in Hailey's eyes. She was failing miserably at trying not to be scared. Gutty could find no reassuring words to offer that they would remain safe inside Minno's bag.

"The flowers brought the bees," Minno said. "It was a trap all along."

The banging diminished until only an occasional bee rammed the bag.

"How long will we stay this size?" Gutty asked.

"To be perfectly honest, I don't really know."

"You don't know? What happens if we stay this small forever? A tiny troll, who ever heard of such a thing?"

"Better than being food for those bee-thingies. Gutty, check to see if they're gone."

Gutty shook his head. The flap was closed, the bees were out there and they were safe inside the bag. Nothing should change, at least not for the time being.

Hours passed in silence. Hailey lay at one side of the bag, while Minno lay at the other. Gutty sat between them with his eyes closed. Then he suddenly stood full upright to listen at the flap.

"It's as quiet as night out there," he reported.

"That's it! Where do bees go at night?"

"Home to the wife and kids ... I don't know."

"Back to their hive when the sun sets."

The bag turned dark as the sun left the sky. Gutty now sat across from the girls with his eyes closed. Minno eased to his side so she could carefully remove the brown leaves covering his wound.

"What! No! Who!" Nole yelled as he bolted awake.

Gutty jumped along with Hailey.

"We're safe for now. No thanks to you," Gutty said.

"We're safe where? Gutty, you're healed!" Nole said with amazement upon seeing the wound in Gutty's side completely closed up.

"How did you know about the magic of those leaves?" Gutty asked of Minno.

She inspected the scar carefully before sliding back across the bag to the other side.

"My grampa. How long will it take to reach Auntie Narra?"

"I don't know."

"Why you seeking Antinarra, kid?"

"To rescue my parents. They're in danger."

"You're awfully small to be rescuing your parents," Nole noted.

"What happened to them?" Gutty asked.

"I don't know. All I know is they're in trouble, and I have to save them."

"Save them from what?" Nole pursued.

"I really don't know."

"We really don't have ..." Nole started.

"We will see that you reach Antinarra safely," Gutty finished.

Nole leveled an icy stare Gutty's way. Gutty shook it off. Nole hadn't witnessed what Craveaux intended to do to him. Nole wasn't there when he said he would be. The girls were. Gutty owed them.

"What were they doing to you back there?" Minno asked.

"Craveaux steals the magic found in all the creatures of Ambrosia."

"So you thought you'd what?" Minno pried.

"Collect the bounty and escape before Craveaux could hurt him," Nole clarified.

"Someday the Soma will come. Craveaux will be destroyed and all the creatures saved," Gutty said.

"Yeah. The gr-r-reat Soma," Nole offered, laden with skepticism. "What's that?"

"Only the biggest, meanest troll ever. We will all be saved."

Gutty huffed, closed his eyes, wrapped his arms across his chest and lowered his chin. "We should sleep now."

"Yeah, I'm beat," Nole said as he curled up.

The girls curled up next to each other across from Nole, and within moments, they fell fast asleep.

"Where are we?" Nole whispered.

He received no answer. So he turned to his side, where he fell back to sleep.

After a few hours of silence in the bag, Gutty eased across, gently blowing pollen into Hailey's face from the blue blossom he had tucked away earlier.

Minno, feeling the shift in the bag, awakened in time to witness Gutty's action, but she remained perfectly still.

"For you, little one," Gutty whispered.

Hailey swatted the air and turned over, but she remained asleep while Gutty returned to his side of the bag and closed his eyes. After a few moments Minno returned to sleep.

Sunrise. Minno's bag sat at the side of the rutted path. The flap eased open. Gutty's head popped out. A moment later, it popped right back in.

Inside the bag, Minno awakened with a stretch. She crawled sleepily over to shake Hailey.

"Ten more minutes," Hailey said.

Shocked, Minno shook her again.

Hailey bolted upright.

"Did I just say that?" She screamed so loud Nole bolted up and spun around.

"Oh, my God, I'm talking!" Hailey chimed.

She hugged Minno.

"Unbelievable! Your bag is amazing! I can speak, world. Everybody just shut up and listen to me. Ha, I always wanted to be able to say that."

Gutty smiled. Nole rolled his eyes.

"That's great. But we're still trapped. What do you say about that?" Minno asked.

"How about, I'm hungry, thirsty and I have to ... I don't suppose this thing comes with a Porta-Potty?"

"Great. We need to get out of here," Nole said.

"Good news. Bees are gone. You are a smart little girl," Gutty said, patting Minno's head.

"Don't call me little girl. I hate that."

Suddenly the bag vaulted skyward to be tossed about. Hailey screamed!

"What's going on?" Nole yelled.

"Oh, yeah, bad news. Oogly brothers found us."

Nole and Gutty braced to keep from being pummelled about.

12

While Moogly sniffed the bag, Doogly and Foogly sniffed the path.

"It's theirs all right," Moogly concluded.

"Nothing here," Foogly called, advancing further down the way.

"Yeah, here's nothing neither," Doogly said from his location in the flower field. He carefully picked his way around the blossoms, careful to leave them undisturbed, as he knew the repercussions of their magic. The three regrouped a moment later around the bag. Foogly snatched it up and shook it.

"Nothing in it?" Doogly asked.

"Open it," Moogly said.

Doogly ripped it from Foogly. He tried the flap—it held fast.

Inside the bag, all four held the flap closed, praying the Ooglys would not figure out how to get it open.

"They open the flap and we're toast," Minno whispered.

"Toast is a good thing or a bad thing?" Gutty pressed.

"I'm thinking bad, real bad," Nole offered.

"You know, had you hidden the bag amongst the flowers, the Oogly brothers probably would never have found it," Hailey offered.

"I think they would have sniffed it out no matter what," Minno offered in her own defense.

Back outside in the flower field, Moogly ripped the bag from Doogly, then used it to smack him up side his head.

"Let me. Neither of you have brains," Moogly said in that voice that could be so grating.

Moogly inspected the bag on all sides. Afterward, she tugged hard on the flap. The bag refused to open. Frustrated, Moogly shook it like crazy.

"Open up, dank you!" Moogly scowled.

"Evidently, you're stupid, too," Doogly said.

That got him whacked again. Then Moogly whacked Foogly for laughing. The three were about to come to fists against each other when they realized fighting would only waste valuable time.

"Why's you gotta do that for?" Foogly whined, rubbing his head.

Inside the bag, the four tumbled about like tossed salad. Hailey reached for Gutty, using his massive size to stabilize herself. Minno was not so lucky; she swiped for Gutty's hand but missed and toppled over.

Nole figured it was best to just keep space between them and try to anticipate the bag's movements. Of course, he had little success initially and soon found himself tumbling onto his head.

Back on the path, the Ooglys sniffed every which way in the hopes of picking up the troll's scent.

"How could we have lost their scent?" Doogly muttered more to himself than to his brothers.

"I don't know, Doogly. Oh, that's right, 'cause you're stupid!" Moogly said.

As a form of apology, Doogly offered Moogly biscuits from a bag he kept slung over his shoulder. She ripped them from him, passed them around and while they chomped down their breakfast, they all tried to figure out why they couldn't pick up the girls' scents.

The bag settled into quiescence.

Inside, Minno tried to hide her concern.

"Tell me you have a plan," Hailey said.

"I'm working on it," Minno offered.

The bag shook for a few seconds then settled upright.

The beginnings of a plan started to take root inside her head.

"We have to do something! We have to do something!" Hailey chimed in, with a voice close to screeching.

"I heard you the first time, I heard you the first time," Minno replied, mimicking Hailey's newfound voice.

"I know. I just like saying it. Now that I can talk, I'm going to talk about everything."

"Great ... just what we need right now," Nole muttered.

"By the way, how we gettin' home? My fosters probably called the cops after they sobered up," Hailey offered more as conversation than with an expectation of a response.

"How long will we stay this size?" Gutty asked.

"What do you mean *this size*?" Nole queried.

"I don't really have answers right now," Minno offered. Her tone made Hailey very uneasy. If Minno had no answers, none of them had answers.

"You don't know? You don't know? What happens if we stay this small, like forever?" Hailey persisted.

"Your repeating things is getting annoying. Besides, can we just solve one problem at a time?"

"What is *this size*?" Nole persisted. Suddenly, he found it difficult to swallow when he realized where they were.

"He smells really bad. Oops! I said that out loud, didn't I," Hailey said when the bag shifted, knocking her into Gutty.

"Me, little one? Smell bad?" Gutty said, fractured by her frankness.

Gutty sniffed.

"My name's Hailey! I've never been able to say that before. It's Hailey. Hi, I'm Hailey. Hailey here. Meet Hailey. And don't you forget that," she responded to Gutty, then she turned her attention to Minno. "I don't suppose that leather book your grandfather read from told you how to get out of this?"

"You're babbling. I can't think when you're babbling," Minno retorted.

"Oh, now it's babbling? First, it's the repeating thing, now it's the babbling thing."

"We're in your ..." Nole pondered out loud.

Outside the bag, the Oogly brothers sampled the ground, hoping to capture the girls' scent as they spread out along the upper ridge of a ravine that cut a jagged path back into the forest. Foogly led the trio on a descent into the belly of the ravine, while Doogly continued across the expanse to sniff the other side. Moogly still clutched the bag while working close to the ground, hoping something might present itself.

Inside, Gutty struggled at the flap while jostling about. He had to keep it closed until the exact right moment, or they would lose their element of surprise. It became imperative that the Oogly brothers remain unaware of their whereabouts. And of course, Minno's plan had to work.

"You sure this will work?" Nole asked. He was anything but confident in what Minno had just laid out.

"And if it doesn't?" Hailey chimed in. Fear grew in her eyes when she considered just how vulnerable they were in their present condition.

"We cross that bridge when we come to it," Minno responded, trying to sound in control, which she wasn't. Yet she hoped they wouldn't recognize that fact until she gave her plan a try. She actually had no idea if her crazy scheme could work. She also had no backup plan, should this one go sour.

"We're at a bridge!" Gutty chimed. "My cousin lives under a bridge. He can help us. I'll stick my head out to call him."

Without thinking, Gutty reached to open the flap.

"No!" Minno, Hailey and Nole all screamed in unison.

Everything stopped for a long moment. Then they all took deep breathes simultaneously. Once Minno's plan went into motion, there'd be no stopping it.

"I don't have a sword. We're unarmed," Nole said.

"Not exactly ..." Minno offered.

Outside the bag, Moogly worked the northern ledge of the ravine alone. The bag scraped along the ground while she sniffed at the edge of the undergrowth, hoping to detect even the slightest scent of any of them. All she needed was a trace left on a leaf or twig, and she'd have enough to determine in which direction they had headed.

"Stop! I got something. They came this way," Moogly called out to her brothers.

It was at that exact moment that the bag flap flipped open and Minno, who had climbed up Gutty inside the bag, leapt out. She landed a few feet from a crouching Moogly.

Moogly turned, coming eye-to-eye with a full-size Minno. Before Moogly could strike, Minno yanked the bag free while shoving Moogly over the ledge into the ravine.

"Now!" Minno yelled.

Gutty came through the open flap next, inflating back to his nine-foot frightened size. Next came Nole. He hit the ground in a fighting stance, not knowing what he would have to face the moment he returned to his full size. Hailey followed; she found herself staring right at Gutty's butt.

"They're here! I've got 'em," Moogly yelled, scrambling back up the ravine wall, not realizing she actually didn't have them at all. She tried to level her spear at Minno while getting back to her feet.

As the spear came up, Nole grabbed it below the tip. Using it like a pole vault, he swung Moogly back into the ravine.

"No, you don't!" Nole said smiling. It was almost too easy to dispose of the Oogly. "Run!" he added just before Foogly jumped onto his back, forcing him to the ground.

Minno took the lead, slipping her bag over her shoulder and grabbing onto Hailey's hand as she passed. Gutty lumbered up behind them, using his girth as a shield, in case the Ooglys launched their spears.

Doogly, across the ravine and a dozen paces behind them, closed quickly on a parallel track. The open expanse of the ravine now separated them, so they figured Doogly was no threat. Or so it seemed.

Nole nailed Foogly with a sharp punch to the jaw that sent him tripping backward in the mushy dirt. As he went down, Foogly took hold of exposed roots to pull himself right back up.

But Nole had returned to his feet and broke into a sprint to catch up with the others. He advanced to the lead with the girls behind him, and Gutty at his side. Neither realized at that moment Hailey had stumbled, surrendering her hand contact with Minno.

Minno looked back as Hailey slowed.

"Hurry," Minno cried out to her friend.

Doogly, still across the ravine, yanked down a drooping vine that extended over the expanse. Lifting his feet, he launched himself to swing over the ravine. He landed a few paces behind Hailey. Before Hailey could react, Doogly snagged a fistful of hair and yanked her to the ground.

Further up the ravine ridge, Minno turned to go back. But Moogly's crossbow quarrel quivered into the tree bole beside her. Nole reached back to snag her arm.

"We have to go," Nole said.

"No. I have to save her," Minno cried out.

"Run, Minno! Save yourself," Hailey called out.

By this time Moogly arrived to reinforce her brother.

"Now is not a time to try anything foolish," Nole counseled.

"Hailey, it's gonna be all right," Minno called before dashing off to catch up with Gutty, who had continued to run for fear they might be able to take him down with a bevy of quarrels, as he proved by far to be the largest target within their range.

A few strides later the three disappeared over a thatchy rise.

Back at the ravine, Foogly sniffed Hailey as Doogly watched their bounty get away once again.

Doogly bared his discolored teeth at her.

"Um ... gross. Could you not do that? And get your grimy hands off me. When was the last time you bathed ... with soap? Or should I not ask?"

"Don't worry. Theys ain't gonna be free for long," Foogly laughed.

Moogly used the moment to draw Doogly away from Hailey and Foogly.

"We need to report this to Craveaux," she said.

"Yessum, that bag's magic is plenty powerful," Doogly said.

Doogly carefully removed a black hummingbird from the pouch over his shoulder. The bird wore a Chogga—a silver metal band around its neck that bound it in servitude to the high minister. Only Craveaux's power could remove the band. And once in place, Craveaux quite easily doled out punishments upon the wearer.

Doogly held the delicate creature to his face.

"High Minister Craveaux, we captured one of the girls. The other, and that stinking troll, got away. But we'll have them soon enough," he said slowly and distinctly to the bird.

"What about the power in the bag?" Moogly asked.

"He doesn't need to know about the bag," Doogly responded.

His message complete, Doogly set the hummingbird free to ascend above the trees.

Hailey took advantage of that distracted moment. While the three watched the hummingbird depart, she jabbed a fierce elbow into Foogly's ribs. When he buckled, she yanked her arm free and bolted for the trees, kicking up dirt with each terrified stride.

But Doogly's reach was quick enough to snare her collar.

"Not so fast, you're our bait," he said. His smile sent her stomach into convulsions.

A good mile from the ravine, Minno paused at a rotting log while Nole watched their wake. She felt like she was going to wretch. They had captured her friend. She couldn't go on without doing something.

"This is all my fault," she said.

"You're right. Let's get moving. They'll hunt us down. They're sniffers. It's what they do," Nole said.

"Yeah, well, sniff this! We're going back."

Gutty, who had remained silent, yielded to his urge to speak.

"I have a better plan. I will go back. I will give them what they want, so you girls and Nole can escape. It is my bounty they want, not your friend."

"I can't let you do that," both Minno and Nole said in unison. They looked at each other. Could they both have said it for the same reason? Minno wondered why Nole would suddenly care.

"What will they do to her?" Minno asked.

"Return her to Craveaux. He will want her now. You cannot long keep secrets from the high minister," Gutty said.

Minno stepped off at a determined march back the way they came.

"Then we need to get moving," she said.

She had no idea how to effectively utilize this bag her grandpa had given her, but there had to be a way to use it to save her friend.

"They'll be expecting us," Nole called out, hoping that alone might induce Minno to abandon some poorly-conceived plan to save her friend.

Gutty glared at Nole.

"What?" was all Nole could offer.

Gutty set out with long strides to catch up to Minno. When he did, he stopped her in her tracks.

"I am here because of you and your friend. I won't let them harm either of you," he said.

"Fine!" Nole said loudly. He shifted to the forefront of both of them.

"I'm not going to let it come to that. If anyone's to blame, it's me. I should've abandoned our plan the moment we ran into the Oogly brothers on the road to the fortress. If I had done that, nothing like this would have happened, and your friend would be safe right now," Nole added.

Gutty raised a suspicious brow. Nole wasn't known for taking responsibility for his actions.

The troll hunter steered them down a path leading in a direction different than that required to rescue Hailey.

"Where we going?" Minno asked with rising anger in her voice.

"If we're taking on the Ooglys, we need to outsmart 'em," Nole offered.

"They don't seem that smart to me," Minno replied.

"They're smart enough," Gutty added as the three disappeared into the undergrowth.

13

A pensive Craveaux sat in a high-backed crystalline chair in his private chamber. Before him two unkempt mop-haired troll hunters presented a string of Haama-gnomes shackled together at the ankles and the wrists. Enmity flashed between Craveaux and the prisoners while the high minister studied the dwarfish half-man, half-gerbil creatures with flopping ears and hunchbacks. They stood no taller than a nine-year-old, but they were noted for their lightning speed and uncanny agility. It was indeed rare in the kingdom that hunters could capture one or two, let alone a string of six.

No one inside the chamber moved for a long moment. Then Sickly came forward to whisper into Craveaux's ear. The high minister smiled as he listened.

The Haama-gnomes giggled.

"This is truly a fine catch, though it appears a few are below the legal size limit," Craveaux stated.

"High m-m-minister, we c-c-captured all s-s-s, s-s-s," a troll hunter started. Failing to deliver the word, he instead raised six fingers, "t-t-together," he finally finished.

Fearing the wrath of an angry ruler, his partner cut in to quiet him. The irascible Craveaux lost patience easily with his subjects, and the troll hunter did not wish his partner to suffer a beating for his affliction. At least not with so much bounty at stake.

"We believed the danger too great if we released the undersized ones," he said. His smile was absent his front teeth, both upper and lower.

Again the Haama-gnomes giggled.

"Ya dang right. We'd chewed off your legs to the knees, then made you run around on your stumps," the eldest Haama-gnome stated. He sported tan and white facial hair rimming ruby red lips that he pursed in defiance. The blood-stained, ruffled fur around his face indicated he had put up a noble fight preceding his capture.

Sickly leaned in close to Craveaux's ear once again.

"Quite the ugly things, but they are entertaining, and they do surrender a fair amount of magic, high minister," Sickly mentioned.

Craveaux contemplated the words. They needed every drop of magic they could get their hands on.

"You make a valid point, Sickly. After we've drained them, they can be ground up into spices. It's said they give even the sourest man a sense of humor," Craveaux replied.

The high minister chuckled to himself. When he looked at Sickly, Sickly chuckled likewise.

"A fair bounty it is then," Craveaux ordered.

"I say it's time we hoist our own petard," the smallest Haama-gnome said.

"I agree. He's asking for it, so let's give it to him," another chimed in, his voice cracking.

"Yeah, let's do it," the last one on the end of the Haama-gnome string added. His was the deepest, and meanest, voice of the creatures.

In unison the Haama-gnomes began rapidly gulping air. Each gulp caused their bellies to expand a little further.

"Hey, chuckle brain Craveaux, this one's for you," another Haama-gnome chided. He stood at the opposite end of the string and next to the stuttering troll hunter.

"*Ready!*"

The Haama-gnomes arched back.

"*Aim!*"

Their faces turned blood red as they prepared.

"*Fire!*"

The Haama-gnomes all belched in rapid succession, releasing long billowing bursts, like fog horns sounding at regular intervals. Then the odd creatures giggled in unison.

The troll hunters standing on either end of the Haama-gnome string nearly fainted as a gray stink cloud wafted into the air around them. The two gagged and coughed, covering their noses while the Haama-gnomes all congratulated each other for a job well done. The creatures seemed impervious to the horrible miasma saturating the air.

"Wait for it," the oldest Haama-gnome said.

In the next moment the full force of the Haama-gnome attack reached Craveaux. When it did, the high minister clamped his nose with one hand, wrapping his arm over his lower face with the other.

"Thank you very much, everybody. We certainly enjoyed being here," another Haama-gnome said.

Sickly wavered. He clung to the chair's armrest to keep from going down. When he breathed in, the old man's eyes bugged out like bulging fish eyes while he gagged.

The Haama-gnomes giggled their infectious childish laugh once again.

"I award the bounty for all six to these brave hunters. Get them away from here!" Craveaux rushed out, muffled through the arm of his robe.

"Brave hunters! Ha! Here, have another round on us!" another Haama-gnome yelled as the hunters tugged them reluctantly out.

"Fire at will!"

Six more rapid-fire belches wafted into the room on their departure. Their raucous giggling echoed into the corridor as the troll hunters yanked them away.

Once the air cleared of the Haama-gnome attack, a black, silver-banded hummingbird zipped in through the window to hover beside Craveaux, who could finally remove his arm from his face and unclamp his nose.

The high minister slid forward in his chair, excited that he might receive news of the girls' capture. He listened intently as the hummingbird recited the message verbatim.

Craveaux's face fell.

"...the other one and that stinking troll got away. We will have them soon enough," the hummingbird repeated in Doogly's voice as it had been perfectly recorded.

"What about the power in the bag?" came next in Moogly's voice.

"He doesn't need to know about the bag." Doogly's voice concluded the message.

Those final words both infuriated and exhilarated Craveaux. The high minister launched like a rocket out of his chair, swatting at the hummingbird as if to kill the messenger.

"The bag! Of course, Craveaux should have known. That little girl has the dragon wing. That is why she protected it so. You are clever, Desrilian, but not clever enough," he muttered while pacing.

His mind swirled in a thousand directions at once. Could it be that the most powerful magic in the kingdom was within his reach? Could Desrilian really have erred? How can he trap those little girls to retrieve their bag? For ten years he's waited and planned for the moment when he would exact his revenge against his nemesis. Unconsciously, Craveaux rubbed the scars marring his face. He would get his chance to settle the score.

The high minister tightened his robe before storming from the chamber. Much to do, little time with which to accomplish it. Wherever those little girls came from, he had to be certain he removed any opportunity for them to return.

In the corridor, two waiting sycophants scurried like mice to get behind him.

"Did you tell them, Desrilian, that no one hides from Craveaux for long? Did you?" Craveaux scowled aloud, though he clearly meant the words only for himself.

"High minister?" a sycophant risked to inject when he failed to understand Craveaux's mumbling.

"Shut up! Leave me, useless twitters," the high minister snarled with vicious intent.

The sycophants tripped over each other to be the first to escape Craveaux's sight—and firing range.

14

The Oogly brothers slept in the quiet of a forest hollow, curled around a dwindling fire. A dozen paces separated one from another. The narrow sliver of moon washed the clearing in a faded gray. Occasionally a snore broke the stillness, as did the howl from a night beast lurking somewhere in the distant darkness.

"Hailey," came as a faint whisper on the wind.

At first, nothing in the small makeshift camp stirred. Then Hailey opened her eyes—she had been awake—just lying there, hoping her friend would not abandon her with these foul, creepy, smelly, sniffing, ugly man-creatures.

Could it be? Or had she just imagined it? Hailey's heart raced. *Please don't be a dream*, a voice inside her head pleaded, desperate to be free.

After another moment without movement, Hailey risked to lift only her head, hoping for a glimpse of who had whispered her name. Excitement rushed through her. Minno had returned.

Hailey froze. Moogly, sleeping closest to her, lifted her head, reluctantly drawing open drowsy eyes and sampling the air.

Panic seized Hailey's pounding heart. If Minno were there, they would smell her and leap to their feet, ready to fight. But instead,

Moogly returned to her slumber, curling tighter and closer to the flickering flames.

But did that mean Minno wasn't there? She hadn't come back. Was it just Hailey's own desperate mind playing tricks on her, making her suffer all the more?

"Don't move. We have a plan," came from a thicket of drooping pine beyond her head.

Oh, my God, Hailey thought, she's saved.

But wait.

Great. Another of Minno's plans. This one had better be better than the last one. That's how she came to be here in the first place.

Hailey dared not shift to locate Minno's position. Anything she did might alert her captors to her friend, then both would become prisoners. A part of Hailey wanted to yell for Minno to run and remain free. Another part prayed she would not. Minno was Hailey's only hope of escaping these mean men.

Very slowly Hailey elevated a leash restraining her to Moogly.

"Please, Minno, see this," she said so faintly that she thought the words came only in her mind.

Moogly remained still. So, for the moment, Hailey and Minno were safe.

Yet neither girl detected the green glowing eyes hovering in the black of a thorny crudberry bush just beyond the clearing. The eyes watched without blinking, without moving.

Minno, Nole and Gutty studied the Ooglys from the crest of a rise overlooking the forest glade where the four slept.

"How do we get her off the leash?" Minno risked.

"I'm working on that," Nole answered. He hadn't factored that into his plan. What seemed, at first, like a simple rescue had become more complicated. And Nole had never faced the Ooglys in a straight-on fight. He didn't think this was the best time to try either. One Oogly he could handle, two maybe, but three at once might be insurmountable. Gutty was too frightened to be of any assistance, and the girls were no match for even a single Oogly.

Gutty refused to fight, as trolls subscribe to only peace and tranquility despite their massive size, which on the other hand, is most suitable for fighting, along with their, at times, fierce-looking faces. Gutty could be a great asset in a fight, but he would never betray his subscription.

"Great," was all Minno could offer to inspire the floundering troll hunter.

A short time later, in the fading darkness that precedes the dawn, Minno crept silently amongst the sleeping Ooglys. She eased herself to the ground, keeping her knees off the dirt. There she carefully wrapped a vine around Doogly's ankles.

He stirred only slightly and never opened his eyes.

With that task completed, she allowed herself a deep breath before slowly bringing herself over her feet.

So far, so good.

Now she could only hope the rest of their plan might work. She signaled Gutty with a waving arm.

In the next moment, Gutty pounded the down the hill, screaming in the meanest voice he could muster.

The jarring noise jolted the Ooglys awake!

Confused, and at the same time frightened, they scrambled to gain their feet. Their heads spun in all directions, trying to assess exactly what was happening around them.

Minno leapt over a fallen log to Hailey's side, where she kept her friend still while Gutty dashed into the glade to reach the Ooglys.

"Now!" Minno yelled.

On her command, she yanked Hailey to her feet at the same time Moogly, who clutched the leash, sprang to her feet. Gutty swooped in, and with both arms extended, took Hailey under one arm, securing Moogly under the other.

Ten paces away, a disoriented Doogly lunged for the girls. But the vine tangled his legs, toppling him face first into the dirt.

"Run," Minno commanded Gutty, who placed his back to the clearing, seeking the quickest path to the rise, making sure to use the glare of an awakening sun to his advantage. Running into the sun would make it impossible for the Ooglys to launch arrows accurately at them. That part of Nole's plan worked flawlessly.

Foogly sprang to his feet, leveling a spear at Minno. Just as he did, Nole popped up from behind, knocking the spear away before flipping Foogly into a thorny crudberry bush. The Oogly cried in agony, picking prickly thorns from his arms and back.

In those two precious minutes when the sun shed its new light upon them, the three had rescued Hailey and raced for the top of the rise.

Once at the crest, Gutty stopped first. He turned back while holding Moogly out, while Minno ripped the leash free. She then sidestepped out of the way. But Nole was still climbing, forcing Gutty to hold a thrashing Moogly until the troll hunter cleared the path.

Doogly scrambled up the rise first, closing in with every pumping stride.

"Not yet," Minno cautioned.

Nole was almost there. But Doogly advanced within reach, and Foogly, while whimpering from his pain, fell in behind his brother.

"Let him go!" Nole yelled. He crested the rise, racing past Minno.

Gutty released Moogly like a log rolling downhill. She tumbled into Doogly and Foogly, sending all three back into the clearing where they started.

The foursome bolted into a dense thicket of pine, where they kept running as fast as they could.

Not far from the glade Minno stopped them, taking advantage of the entangling mesh of low hanging limbs.

"Some plan. How long ya think it's gonna take them to catch up? Whoa, what is that stink?" Hailey said, catching her breath.

"Stop talking and step all over Gutty's feet," Nole commanded.

Hailey just looked at him. He was serious.

"Are you nuts!"

"Just do it, please," Minno chimed in.

"Yo-o-kay," Hailey replied, complied, and without a second's more delay, they were running again.

"Ecch! What is that?" Hailey complained.

"Dragon stuff. You know, what dragons leave behind. It masks our scent," Gutty informed her while he jogged beside her.

"Dragon poop! I'm *wearing* dragon poop! Totally gross."

"Here they come, run faster," Nole commanded with a tremor in his voice.

The Ooglys were still some distance behind, but they had a bead on them. They ran at full pelt.

"We're running out of trees," Minno yelled, trying to squash the panic in her voice.

They spilled into a sprawling meadow crammed with dried six-foot corn stalks and equally high straw-colored grass. The growth quickly swallowed up the girls and Nole. But Gutty's head bobbed above the corn stalks.

Minno stopped them in the middle of the field.

"This isn't going to work. They can see him," she said.

"All right. A little flaw in the escape plan," Nole admitted.

In the meantime, Gutty hunched over as low as he could go, hoping he too might disappear. It almost worked. But still the tip of his head remained in view. And that was enough for the Ooglys to know they were still on the trail.

"Hel-lo. There's a nine foot flaw in the plan," Hailey added.

"Gutty, listen to me. This is very important. You don't need to be frightened anymore. Can you do that?" Minno begged.

"Oh, sure," Gutty replied, shaking his head otherwise.

"Really?" Hailey said, surprised.

"No. Not really."

"I won't let anything happen to you. I have my bag. I'll can stop them in their tracks if they come too close," Minno continued. She took Gutty's hands into hers.

"You must believe in me. Our safety depends on it."

She gazed deeply into the troll's eyes. Gutty nodded.

Gutty began shrinking. In less than thirty seconds, his size matched the girls. He became hidden in the grass and corn stalks. Nole led them in a wide zigzag pattern, knowing the Ooglys couldn't capture their scent, and hoping to that it was now impossible for the Ooglys to detect exactly which way they went.

"We need a forest's help. This way," Gutty said.

"I seed 'em, brothers," Foogly yelled. The words came from somewhere not far enough behind them.

After more running, the corn stalks thinned. The four of them became visible again. Less than ten minutes behind, the Ooglys emerged from the tall grass. They quickened their pursuit, clustering back together into attack formation.

"We're not gonna make it," Hailey yelled.

Suddenly the Ooglys stopped dead in their tracks. They reversed course to scramble like scurrying rats, racing back into the tall grass.

"They're giving up!" Minno screamed triumphantly.

"Why?" Nole asked, suspicious. The Ooglys disappeared. The Ooglys don't abandon a bounty.

"Uh, oh," Gutty said, back at his nine-foot height.

The girls stared in stunned silence at the cloud-infested sky.

Dragons! Huge, iridescent green, terrifying dragons. The pair of twenty-foot creatures broke through the cloud ceiling in a circling descent—heading directly for them!

"This can't be good. See what you get for stepping in their poop!" Hailey stammered, frozen in her tracks.

The dragons gangly size caused them to be clumsy in flight. Their expansive wing span, though quite adapted to gliding, proofed less effective for flapping and quick maneuvers. They were too easily spotted in the open skies from great distances, making it near impossible for them to sneak up on Palladins on the ground.

As Gutty came sprinting by, he scooped Hailey into his arms and beat feet for the trees. Nole lifted Minno with an arm under her shoulder while trailing Gutty. But Nole advanced no more than five steps before crumpling to the ground, falling fast asleep atop Minno.

"Help me!" Minno screamed. She squirmed to make her way out from beneath the troll hunter. But she couldn't abandon him. She tugged with all her strength, trying to bring him to his feet.

The safety of the forest seemed a mile away, though they were only slightly more than fifty yards off. Gutty released Hailey to return to bring Nole into his arms.

"Go for the trees. Do not stop for anything," he commanded the girls.

In moments Minno and Hailey sprinted ahead of Gutty in their mad dash for the safety of the forest. Fear and panic flooded their heads. They were both too terrified to breathe. The dragons were huge. Gutty pounded his feet into the soft dirt, pumping his legs as hard as he could. His heart rammed against his chest. A dragon's shadow cast over him. He wanted to scream but couldn't. He dared not glance back for fear he might stumble, causing both to become dragon food.

The low hanging umbra swallowed up Hailey first, with Minno a step behind. Gutty broke through the branches with Nole safely in his arms a few seconds after Minno, and fortunately for them, a few seconds ahead of the plunging dragons. Once ensconced within the trees, Gutty stopped first. Minno and Hailey only stopped after they saw Gutty resting on a log.

15

The forest became deathly quiet. The dragons had ceased their pursuit and returned aloft. The girls, the troll and Nole had slipped away using the security of entangling limbs. Dragons became extremely vulnerable within a forest's woody mesh, and therefore, remained in open fields and upon the mountaintops. Their sprawling wingspans made it near impossible for them to achieve flight within the confining constraints of the woods. The Palladins knew that and over time had devised tricks and traps to lure dragons into woody places, where capture could be more easily achieved. Palladins had little incentive to kill the dragons, since dead dragons yielded no magic to the high minister, and thus, no bounty to them.

Gutty stopped them to rest on a fallen log waist-high to Minno. Overhead the thick crown canopy virtually guaranteed the dragons would pursue them no further. The sleeping Nole had become too heavy for Gutty to continue to run. While there they were safe, very little sunlight reached them, creating ominous dark spots in the forest.

"Dragons won't come after us now," the troll churned out between gasps.

"How could you let this happen? What's the matter with you? Did you unscrew your brain or something?" Hailey hammered out, all in one forceful burst.

"Me? How can that be my fault?" Minno replied.

"Sorry. I just wanted to say that. It is so great to talk. I am so jazzed. What do we do now?" Hailey pumped the words out as fast as she could think of them.

"You keep asking like I somehow know," Minno replied.

Nole bolted awake, scrambling to his feet, poised to fight.

Both girls just looked to him.

"What?" he started. He gazed at their surroundings. "I got us here, didn't I?" But here was, in essence, the middle of nowhere when it came to reaching Antinarra. Nole, like Gutty, hoped they would hear something soon from the troll's cousins.

Gutty said nothing.

"Where is here?" Minno pressed.

"Whoa. I can't believe you've found a stench worse than dragon poop. What is that horrible smell? It's, like, all around us," Hailey commented.

"The Forest of Perpetual Stink."

"I can see why you'd call it that."

"Haama-gnome territory," Nole warned. "You don't want to know," he added off Minno's inquiring look.

"Just hope we don't run into them," Gutty added.

"*The sun'll come out to-morrow, bet your bottom dollar that to-morrow ... come what may,*" Hailey sang then ceased abruptly when Minno's glare stabbed her.

"I'm thinking, bad time to sing," Minno harped.

"I love to sing. I think I have a great voice. What do you think?"

"I think we should eat," Gutty said, busy scanning the treetops.

"No Yassah fruit. I'm not eating worms. There has to be some normal food in this land," Hailey said.

"Don't suppose you have real food here? Like hamburgers, french fries, banana cream pies?" Minno rattled off.

She got blank stares from Gutty and Nole, who exchanged their own look of confusion.

Without answering, Gutty, who had returned to his unfrightened size, lifted Hailey into the trees to pick huge red apples. It would take both of Hailey's hands to even hold them. With his fear abating, Gutty fell short of reaching the ripe fruit.

"Can't you make yourself sprout up a little more," Hailey begged.

Even stretching full length, and precariously teetering in Gutty's grasp, she failed to reach the lowest hanging orbs.

"I can't do it on command." He hoisted her as far as he could.

"Oh, no, get me down! There's a Haama-gnome!" Hailey screamed in terror.

In response, Gutty spurted up two feet. Hailey knocked free three apples in rapid-fire succession. Two fell into Minno's waiting arms. A third landed at her feet.

Nole refused to assist. Instead, his eyes worked the forest. Nothing moved that heightened his suspicion, nor were any sounds detected to raise an alarm. Nonetheless, Nole remained uneasy.

Minno caught the fourth apple to drop. But a fifth apple went rogue, rolling away downhill to disappear into a tall hedgerow of bushes. Behind the leafy wall, a huge gray rabbit paw stopped the fruit.

While the four lounged beneath the apple trees, chomping on lunch, Hailey subtly pointed out Nole's agitation to Minno.

"Do you like?" Gutty asked.

"They're great. I've never seen apples this big back home," Hailey offered.

"Where is home?" Nole queried.

"Let's just say we're not from around here," Minno cut in.

"I figured that much out," Nole said.

"Why is reaching Antinarra so important?" Gutty pried.

"My gramps said Auntie Narra's the key to finding my parents."

Gutty whistled, bringing a green hummingbird in hovering near his head.

"Jaswor, anything on Antinarra? It's real important," he said.

Nole watched the hummingbird climb into the trees. A moment later, three black Chogga-clad hummingbirds swooped in out of nowhere to viciously attack the green bird. Their attack ceased when the green bird floundered, fluttering lifelessly to the ground.

"What's wrong, Nole?" Minno asked. His actions seized her curiosity.

Nole decided at that moment it was best the girls remain unaware of what just happened. Seemed the high minister had dispatched every force under his control to oppose them. Now Nole knew why their earlier messengers never returned.

"Time to move out. Hanging around anywhere too long is dangerous." He never took his eyes off the surrounding umbrage. He saw nothing, heard nothing; but nonetheless, he felt danger closing in on them.

"What? No. It's so peaceful here. No Ooglys, no dragons. Can't we stay until one of those birds comes back?" Hailey said.

"It's too peaceful. I'm worried. We move. I take point."

"Yes, commander," Hailey returned with an accompanying mock left-handed salute.

Nole ignored her chiding while moving out down a forest path. His vigilant eyes swept side to side, peering as deep into the growth as possible.

"How old are you, Gutty?" Hailey worked up the nerve to venture.

"Let's walk faster," Nole commanded.

He broke into a half run. Gutty and the girls lagged further behind within moments. Gutty gave no answer to her question.

"Hey, that's not a walk. That's a run. Why didn't you say, let's run. You said let's walk faster. There is a difference, you know," Hailey complained.

Her words brought Nole's angry glare back around. But something on the edge of his vision stopped him in his tracks.

"So, those tubes were draining your magic?" Minno asked.

"Stealing our magic makes Craveaux stronger against us. It also protects him from us. But unless it is drained very slowly, it dies with us," Gutty said.

"Sshh!" Nole injected.

"Do all creatures here have magic?" Hailey asked, turning her volume down to a whisper.

All stopped. Their eyes followed Nole's stare. The troll hunter's face turned deathly pale.

"Dragons?" Hailey queried.

"Worse," Nole replied.

The hair on Minno's neck stood on end.

"Worse?" she swallowed.

Hailey clung to Minno, who clung to Gutty ... who pointed.

A gray and white rabbit head popped out from the undergrowth twenty feet from them. It stared at Nole with hatred in dark soulless eyes that did not blink, did not waver.

Nole, though visibly intimidated, shifted himself between the girls and the rabbit, while reaching for a sword that wasn't there. He had never felt more vulnerable than at that moment. He knew he could do little, other than to stand between the danger and the girls. Even Gutty refused to move at the sight of the creature.

"Oh, it's a cute little rabbit," Hailey said, assuming the lead as if she would deal with whatever came next.

"You might want to stay back," Minno cautioned.

Walking upright, the five-foot rabbit emerged to take over the path. It wore leather chest armor, while wielding a honed double-edged sword.

"Yeah, you should go first," Hailey said, slipping in behind Nole.

A dozen more rabbits, all armed and armored, barricaded the path.

"Haama-gnomes?" Minno risked in a whisper.

"I wish. Forbits," Nole responded in an equally soft voice.

"This is gonna be a problem, isn't it?" Minno added.

Nole swallowed. He nodded slightly to acknowledge her. His eyes never left the lead rabbit on the path.

The moment between them lingered until . . .

Gutty and Nole bowed in respect.

"We mean no harm. Allow us to pass without confrontation and no one gets hurt," Nole offered, with the most authoritative voice he could muster. Only a fool would attempt to bluff their way through a Forbit confrontation. Then again, Nole had been a fool much of his life.

All thirteen rabbits laughed at once. Not the funny 'ha, ha' laughter, more the 'that's funny, come and try' laughter meant to strike terror more than to diffuse tension.

The lead rabbit advanced one step.

"A Palladin who means no harm. And unarmed at that." The leader spoke with a thick Scottish brogue.

"You noticed, did ya?" Nole said.

"Good move," Hailey slipped in.

"You know full well no Palladin passes through this forest unchallenged."

"We're not Palladins," Minno offered, once she got over the shock of sword-wielding rabbits that spoke. Of course, back at the waterfall the fish spoke, so why shouldn't the rabbits?

"Really? Then you're what, trolls?" the rabbit said.

His band behind him laughed.

"We're Californians," Minno responded.

The rabbits mumbled amongst themselves as if conferring to determine exactly what was a Californian.

"Perhaps you could just remain quiet. Let me do the talking," Nole said out the side of his mouth.

"Oh, yeah, that's been working so well 'til now," Minno shot back.

"Advance, Cal-i-for-ni-ans," the rabbit leader ordered.

So far not a single rabbit had reached for their sword, which offered hope that they might find a way past the clan without a fight.

The four started forward.

"Not you, troll," the rabbit leader added.

Gutty froze where he stood.

The girls continued two more steps. But Nole's advance brought out the swords.

The girls and Nole stopped.

"Look, Mr. ..." Minno started, her voice meant to convey caution absent the fear.

"Commander Dulfay. Supreme leader of the Forbit clan and descendant of those that came before," Dulfay corrected.

"Yeah, right, Commander Dulfay, please allow us to pass. It's very important we reach Auntie Narra."

Her words sent the rabbits into another grumbling conference.

"Antinarra?" Dulfay said with genuine surprise.

"My parents, they're in trouble. I must reach them."

One of the rabbits whispered into Dulfay's ear. The commander's face turned to dismay.

Hailey decided she might have more success than either Nole or Minno, since she loved animals and always felt her lack of a voice gave her a special kinship with them. Of course, back home none of them spoke to her nor carried weapons.

"Look, nice cute bunnies with swords, we mean no harm. We'll even pinkie swear if that'll help. Could you just please see your way clear to allow ..." she offered.

"Silence!" Dulfay snapped.

The rabbits' ensuing growls terrified the girls into retreating a step.

"They're not going to let us pass," Nole said. He retreated to a position where he might protect the girls against a Forbit attack.

"Any ideas?" Minno asked.

At least for the moment, the Forbits maintained their distance. Maybe they were frightened of Gutty? Maybe they weren't as tough as they wanted everyone to think? Then again, maybe they were? They all clutched swords and appeared prepared to use them. But surely they'd never attack children.

"Think you can pull fifty carrots from that bag for them to eat?" Hailey asked.

"Ipitzay about the agbay, okay?" Minno cautioned. Her eyes were serious. Saying one wrong thing could heighten the danger, if that were possible at the moment.

"Oh, that's good. Pig Latin. Like they'll never figure that out."

"They don't eat carrots," Gutty added.

"What do they ... oh, ya know what, I don't want to know," Hailey said.

Minno pressed her brain to find a way past sword-wielding rabbits to continue their journey. Oddly enough, they seemed to be at a standoff. They couldn't proceed, and the Forbits chose not to advance upon them.

"Only the most foolish fool would come unarmed with a troll," Dulfay said.

"Exactly. You don't need to fear this foolish fool. Let us pass, we promise no trouble. These little girls must find their parents," Nole offered, detecting a slight opportunity to reason with them.

"What? You, too, with the little girls!" Minno spat back.

"Not now. Please," Nole replied.

"Since *you* are unarmed, the little girls shall pass," Dulfay offered.

"All right. I've had about enough of this little ..." Minno shot in.

"Are you *trying* to get us sliced up?" Nole pressed.

"That's what I'm talking about," Hailey chimed in. She stepped forward.

"*If* you defeat us in a challenge, *which* you most likely cannot," Dulfay added.

Hailey stopped.

"What?" she said, too loud.

Minno seized on an opportunity.

"How about, if we defeat you, you tell us how to reach Auntie Narra." She had nothing to lose at this point. And maybe they would take pity on them and offer up some clue as to where, or how far, they had to go to reach Antinarra. It appeared at the moment they would no longer be allowed to continue with Gutty and Nole.

Instead of an answer, the rabbits laughed.

"If *you* defeat *us*, we'll take you to Antinarra," Dulfay said, believing full well he would never need to deliver on the offer.

"And if we lose?" Minno asked. Her confidence grew, since rather than wielding swords against them, the Forbit clan was negotiating for things far less dire than their lives.

"More the likely. We take the troll," Dulfay said matter-of-factly.

"And that bag," a rabbit soldier beside the commander added.

"And the necklace," another rabbit said from amongst the crowd.

Hailey's hand went to her necklace and the silver band around her neck. She had all but forgotten she had it on. She vowed she would never be without the locket and the only photo she had of her mother.

The girls huddled with Nole and Gutty while the Forbits looked on.

"First of all, tell me these things don't eat trolls. Cuz there's no way I'm letting 'em eat ya, Gutty," Hailey said.

"Thanks."

Minno sized them up.

"They don't really look that big. And we've got you two on our side."

"What is this challenge, anyway?" Hailey asked of Nole.

"How would I know?"

"So, it could, in fact, be impossible to beat them," Hailey added.

"For some reason, Gutty, they want you, so the decision's got to be yours," Minno said. She could see Gutty's mind churning through his fawn-like eyes.

"If it helps you reach Antinarra, then we must try," the troll offered.

He waited for Nole's response. None came. All four knew they would have to face this challenge, and hope they might find a way to save themselves in the process.

The four broke their huddle. Minno advanced, feigning confidence.

"Deal. You win, we get the troll. We win, you take us to Auntie Narra."

Minno chose her words carefully, hoping the Forbits were as dumb as the rabbits in her world. Of course, they didn't look or act like the rabbits in her world.

Commander Dulfay's eyes narrowed. He searched hers.

Could Minno's crazy ploy possibly work?

Dulfay laughed.

"Very funny, *little* girl. We win, *we* get the troll. You win we take you to Antinarra. Did you honestly think Forbits are as dumb as Palladins?"

So that wasn't the smartest thing for Minno to try.

"Yo-kay. I guess they're not," Hailey offered.

But Minno detected the softening in the commander's voice. The truth was that those Forbits had no intention of harming them—Minno was certain of that. She just had to find some way to manipulate the Forbits into setting *all* of them free—even the troll hunter.

"Fine. Have it your way. What about Nole?"

16

At the fringes of an open meadow, in the midst of the Forest of Perpetual Stink, Nole hung upside down from the lowest bough of a tree. Fist-size hemp rope bound him shoulders to waist.

A dozen paces away, the Forbits had stacked their arms and armor, while in the middle of the field the girls and Gutty engaged the rabbits in what seemed like some form of rugby game.

The Forbits tossed a furry oblong ball back and forth, booting it at times, as if attempting to keep it from the girls. When Minno dove for the ball and missed, a Forbit scooped it up and the clan suddenly huddled near midfield.

"Point! We lead one, zero." Dulfay's voice rang out with confidence.

The girls and Gutty crossed to the side of the field to huddle with Nole.

"How did they get a point?" Minno asked.

"Don't look at me. I don't know what's going on," Nole said.

Minno turned to Hailey.

"How would I know? I have no idea how we play this crazy game."

"Okay, fine, follow my lead," Minno instructed.

They broke their huddle, grabbed the ball and mimicked the For-bits' moves, tossing and booting the ball to keep it from the rabbits. Gutty was quick to pitch it to Hailey when it bounced into his hands.

Hailey screamed as the rabbits charged. She flipped it high end-over-end for Minno. A Forbit sprang to the air, narrowly missing the ball.

Suddenly, Minno tossed the ball to Gutty. She threw up her arms in victory.

"Point! One, one," she chimed.

"How could you let them get that?" Commander Dulfay yelled, "Who's supposed to be watching her?" Disgust crept into his words.

"How'd we get a point?" Hailey asked, dashing over to Minno to take the ball.

"No idea," Minno said, shrugging her shoulders. She indicated for Hailey to toss the ball to the Forbits. "They bought it, so let's go for another one."

"Yeah, sure, right," Hailey muttered.

Play progressed back and forth with the Forbits intercepting the ball, kicking it, then flipping it back and forth while hopping skyward. At one point, Hailey dove for the ball but missed it, coming up with a faceful of soft earth.

"Another point. We lead two, one," Dulfay chimed in.

So engaged in their challenge were they, that no one noticed green eyes watching from within the umbrage beyond the stacked armor. Only the two glowing green orbs were visible.

"Time out!" Minno yelled, out of breath and sweating.

Gutty lumbered up.

"Do they even have time-outs?" he asked.

Minno shrugged, but everyone stopped, so she figured they must. Anyway, it worked.

"What's the score?" she called to Dulfay, who gathered his men about twenty yards away at the opposing end of the field.

"Tied. Four, four. Next point wins," Dulfay cautioned, then huddled with his men.

The girls and Gutty again huddled beside Nole.

"All right. We're not doing so bad. We at least tied it up. We just find a way to stop them, then yell point and claim we've won."

"Stop them from what? How do we stop them when we don't even know what they're doing?" Hailey persisted.

"Look, so far they have no idea that we don't know what we're doing," Minno added.

"What about this? You trip them, grab the ball and yell point, we win," Nole offered.

"Is tripping allowed?" Hailey asked.

Everyone shrugged.

At that moment, the Forbit clan broke their huddle, dashing for the middle of the field. Their time-out was over, and they had to hope for the best.

The ball arced into the field. Gutty slid to reach it first. He tossed it to Minno, seconds before the rabbits piled onto him, grinding the huge troll into the dirt.

Minno was off and running, with Hailey on her left flank. As the Forbits peeled off Gutty to take up the chase, Minno flipped the ball to Hailey, who widened the gap between them.

Gutty pulled himself to his knees. When he wiped the dirt from his eyes, he stared at the ground before him. The tip of an ivory-colored egg horn protruded from the dirt. Wild exhilaration swarmed every part of Gutty's aching body. It had to be a sign!

The troll's eyes alighted with child-like excitement. He glanced about before quickly unearthing the egg horn and tucking it into his pants. He made certain no one, especially the Forbits, saw him hide it away.

The girls' screams brought him to his feet. The game was not over. They needed him. He spun about and locked onto them. Just as he did, the ball hurled toward his face.

BAM!

Stunned, Gutty tried to steady himself, while the ball bounced harmlessly on the ground.

The Forbits charged en mass.

"Don't let 'em get it," Hailey yelled. She was too far across the field to help.

The Forbits all launched themselves, ready to pounce. Gutty kicked at the ball as hard as he could. The oblong orb sailed over the charging rabbits as they approached.

Minno was best positioned to receive the ball. Gutty then stuck out his leg, and as the Forbits turned to chase Minno, they all tripped into a pile of flailing rabbit flesh.

Minno lofted the ball to arm's length.

"Point. We win!" she chimed in victory.

The stunned Forbits returned to their feet.

"Ugh! You are all a disgrace. The Forbit clan has never lost a match. Who was covering her? MacLeay!" Dulfay yelled.

Rabbit soldier MacLeay stepped forward, snapping to attention.

"Sir!" McLeay uttered with a sharp salute.

Commander Dulfay smacked him hard across the face. The rabbit soldier never even flinched.

"Okay, dismissed," Dulfay said in such a way as to indicate that the punishment had been doled out, and as such, all was now forgiven.

"Yes, sir. Thank you, sir," Macleay said with a military precision. He returned to the formation of Forbits behind Commander Dulfay.

"How did we do that?" Hailey whispered to Minno.

"*You're asking me?*" was all Minno could reply.

They came together in the middle of the field ... all except for Nole, who remained bound upside down on the tree limb.

"You're good, very good. You defeated us fair and square. We will honor our wager," Dulfay said.

"Then you'll take us to Auntie Narra?" Minno chimed.

Excitement seized her insides. They were going to Antinarra; they were going find her parents. She would soon be reunited with them. She wondered what her mother would look like. Would she be young? Would she be older? Dulfay's words drew her out of her fantasy.

"As agreed, my lady. You have earned the respect and admiration of the Forbit clan. But maybe next time we will defeat you," Dulfay said.

As the group moved together from the field to the stacked armor, the floating green eyes evaporated. The Forbits suited up before forming into two columns and beginning their trek.

"Hey! Hey, what about me? You can't leave me like this," Nole called in a panic. He squirmed with all his might, hoping to break the rope holding him upside down.

Moments later a rabbit soldier bounced up to slice the rope suspending Nole, who then, of course, crashed to the ground on his head.

17

A glum Craveaux sat in the high minister's chamber with his robe open across his chest, making visible the pulsating green light around his neck. His hands clutching the armrests, he seemed to stare at nothing. Overhead, dozens of nymphflies buzzed chaotically about, their bodies a perfect childlike form the length of a man's hand. Gossamer wings, similar to a butterfly's, held them aloft, working back and forth in smooth effortless gyrations. They circled lazily about high enough inside the chamber to remain out of Craveaux's dreaded reach, yet from their vantage point they could see—and hear—all that transpired.

All of sudden Craveaux burst from his chair, throwing his arms up in wild gyrations.

"Sickly!" he screamed as if struck by terrible pain.

The old man stumbled in like life or death hung in the balance. He bowed, clutching his chest to calm his frail racing heart.

"Yes, high minister, what is your bidding, your most high greatness, master of the kingdom ... supreme noble, kind, highest ruler."

"Enough sniveling. Command General Furion to attack the Forbit Clan in the Forest of Perpetual Stink. There he will find the fugitive troll and the two little girls. He is to bring those little girls to me at once."

"The Forbit Clan? Forest of Perpetual Stink. The little girls? Yes, your high ministerness. What of the troll and the Forbits?"

"Dispose of them," Craveaux said dismissively.

"High minister? Surely we need their magic."

"Once Craveaux has that little girl's ba ..." the high minister censored himself. Some things must remain secret, even from the people trusted most. "Craveaux will be the most powerful in the land. Now go!"

Sickly trembled as he bowed his way out of the chamber.

Back in his chair, the high minister ruminated.

"Soon Craveaux will have what he needs to enslave the last of those vile dragons."

As the high minister left his chair to pace in his chamber, the nymphflies formed into a tight circle before fluttering out en mass through the highest window.

18

The Forbit clan led the group through the forest with Nole still bound behind them, followed by the girls, with Gutty trailing at the rear.

As he walked, Gutty's hand drifted toward his pocket as if to make certain his egg horn was still there. After making certain no one was watching, he carefully extracted his find to wipe it clean of all remaining dirt. He admired his newfound treasure in his palm. His smile betrayed his secrecy, causing him to glance around, hoping no one noticed him. If the Forbits learned of his discovery, they would surely seize it from him. He clutched it tightly as he strolled, daydreaming of all the possibilities that might come from his good fortune. He had heard so many success stories and had dutifully listened politely to other fortunate people speak of their good fortune as a result of uncovering an egg horn. Now it was his turn. He wished for only one thing in all his life, and just maybe the egg horn would make it come true. He believed now, beyond any doubt, he would succeed in uniting Minno with her parents.

Hailey turned back to check on him. She smiled. Gutty smiled back, and for a fleeting moment, considered revealing his treasure to her.

"You think the Ooglys are back there?" she asked.

Gutty abandoned his fancy of sharing for fear she might inadvertently let his secret slip. Then trouble would surely follow. He stuffed his egg horn back into his pocket.

"They will pick up our scent ... won't stop until they have us. The bounty on a troll makes a poor man sing with joy. Lives are changed by such good fortune," Gutty said.

Minno used the opportunity to catch up to Commander Dulfay, who still clutched the ball used in their challenge.

"What do you call that game?" she asked.

"Kick the cat," he replied without looking at her.

"The cat?"

"Yes. Filthy, insolent creatures. Only thing they're good for."

At that, the ball transformed into a black scruffy cat that screeched and leapt from Dulfay's hands to dash away into the trees.

"Have no magic, useless creatures."

"How much further ..." Minno ventured.

"Getting close now."

With Nole's hands still bound, a rabbit soldier pulled him along as the sun fell below the peaks of the northern mountains. Their long arduous day was finally coming to an end, and for the first time since arriving in this land, Minno actually felt closer to locating her parents. She thought about what she might say when their eyes first meet. Everything was a terrible jumble inside her brain. She realized she would probably be incapable of speech at that moment, opting instead to throw her arms around her mother's neck to hug her with all her strength.

Gutty suddenly broke from the path, leaping skyward like a very *un*graceful ballerina. He stretched full length, desperate for something floating overhead.

It was a bubble. Hailey spotted it next, then Minno.

"What are you doing?" Hailey asked, irritated and surprised.

"I must get it," Gutty said.

"Huh? It's a bubble."

"There's another one," Minno added.

Gutty swung around to leap after that one instead. When he failed to reach it, he commandeered Hailey onto his shoulders to help him.

"Hurry, get it," Gutty commanded.

"Why? It's a stupid bubble," Hailey replied. Then she realized what she had said. Here in this land a bubble could be something far more important than a mere bubble back home.

Hailey stretched her left hand out while clutching Gutty's head with her right. Her fingers covered his eyes, forcing Gutty to meander off the path into a thicket of towering pine.

"Watch out!" Nole yelled.

Gutty came within inches of whacking a six-foot diameter pine trunk.

In desperation, Hailey leapt from Gutty's shoulders. Her hand touched the floating prismatic orb. When it did, the bubble burst into nothingness.

"*He has found you. Run, Gutty! Soldiers coming. Grave danger,*" a female voice fluttered. The words flowed out of the bubble when Hailey's touch popped it.

Hailey plummeted to the ground, tucking into a roll then into a tumble that brought her right back to her feet.

Gutty looked to Nole, worry consuming the troll's eyes. Fear took over Nole's face.

"What does this mean?" Minno asked.

"It will take time for them to find us. We will get you to Antinarra, I promise," Gutty responded as they hurried to catch up to the Forbits, who were now a good fifty paces in the lead.

"Okay, how does that whole bubble thing work?" Hailey asked.

Gutty looked at her perplexed.

"Do you not use nymphflies where you come from?"

"Use them? I don't even know what they look like," she muttered to herself as she walked.

"They warn us of Craveaux's intentions. The high minister has no idea our spies see and hear every move he makes in his fortress."

As the dying rays of an orange sun faded from view, and darkness settled upon the forest, the group pitched camp for the night in the hollow of a woody thicket. Each sat by themselves: the Forbits taking the periphery of the clearing, acting as sentries; while Gutty, the girls and Nole huddled around a feeble central fire.

The Forbits passed around leathery strips of dried meat, what kind Minno had no idea, and she had no desire to inquire. She and Hailey being famished chewed down every bite, even though it took many minutes to consume their meager dinner.

"I wish they had some real food to eat," Hailey muttered afterward.

"Later, we can have some Schmores, if you like," Gutty said.

"Really?" both girls said in excitement.

"That would be great," Hailey added. The idea of gooey chocolate and marshmallows set her salivating. It would be the first good thing to eat they'd have since coming to this strange land.

"Ask them if I can be unbound," Nole whispered so only Minno could hear.

"No!" Dulfay spat without turning his head.

"I'm thinking the large ears allow them to hear everything we say," Hailey offered to Nole, which brought a displeasing frown from the troll hunter.

After dinner, Gutty settled into the hollow of a giant dead oak tree, with a girl on each side for warmth against the night chill. Fallen leaves blanketed them neck high.

The rabbit band became invisible scattered amongst the undergrowth. Only their soft breathing gave away their presence. Nole, on the other hand, snored with a buzzing resonance impossible to conceal in the still. He curled close to the dying flames overrun by glowing embers.

For a long time the girls stared at a red glow crowning a majestic mountain far in the distance.

"What's that?" Minno asked when she realized sleep was refusing to overtake her. A flood of memories of her grandfather, coupled with thoughts of her parents forced her mind awake.

Tomorrow may be the day. Tomorrow she could be reunited with her parents. She imagined what they might look like; how they would look when she told them she was here. Would they be shocked? Would they smile and cry, like she knew she would when she ran into her mother's arms for the first time. Was her father tall and strong? Would his hug be so tight and loving that it would prevent her from breathing? She didn't care. Just to be with them would be worth all the pain and suffering she endured to reach them.

"Mortus," Gutty told her after a long pause. "A very dangerous place." His inflection conveyed a notion of great suffering there.

"Please tell me we're not going there," Hailey said. Her eyes remained closed.

"No one, save for the bravest Palladin, has ever returned from Mortus to speak of the dread of that place."

Minno moved a little closer to Gutty to partake of more of his body heat.

"Who wants Schmores?" Gutty chimed.

Hailey popped her eyes open in time to watch Gutty snatch a firefly right out of the air. He popped it into his mouth with a satisfied smile."

"Not me," Hailey said, realizing Schmores in this land had neither chocolate nor marshmallow. The very thought of eating live glowing bugs soured her stomach.

Gutty grabbed another to pop into his mouth before closing his eyes.

"It is time we sleep," he said.

"What're you gonna do when you find 'em?" Hailey asked. She couldn't see Minno around the troll, but she knew her friend would be awake. Who could sleep when they were this close?

"I don't know. I'm still not sure I even believe they're alive."

"Hel-lo, we're sleeping beside a nine-foot troll, well not nine feet right now, he's our size now. We're being protected by five-foot rabbits, and hiding out from dragons, not to mention creepy Palladin people hunting us. I think I'd believe just about anything," Hailey said.

"We should sleep," Gutty interrupted.

"What I wouldn't give for a double cheeseburger with chili cheese fries right now," Hailey added.

"What I wouldn't give for a bowl of my grampa's stew."

Silence settled between them for a few moments.

"You think it's legal to keep a troll as a pet?" Hailey asked.

"Here?"

"No. In Blue Lake."

"I don't think we can take him with us when we go back."

"Why? He can't stay here. Craveaux's gonna get him sooner or later."

"He's got Nole."

"Oh, you mean Mr. L double-O oozer."

"Loser doesn't have two Os."

"Whatever. Maybe I can get one of those exotic pet licenses."

"I'm right here. I'm not asleep," Gutty injected.

"Oh, I thought you were," Hailey said.

"I would be, if two little gir ... I mean, young ladies, would cease talking."

Silence resumed for many minutes.

Gutty began to snore, softly at first. Then louder as he fell deeper into his slumber. A yelping howl broke the still, jolting the girls, but leaving Gutty undisturbed. Then shrieks from something lurching about in the trees. The girls pressed closer to the troll for protection.

"I'm jealous, ya know," Hailey said.

"Of?"

"You, getting to hug your parents," Hailey revealed. It slipped out of her tortured soul in a weak moment. She knew *their* relationship would never be the same once Minno reunited with her parents. Right now, at least, they were each alone and needed one another. Not so for long. Minno would have her family. She'd no longer need Hailey, who'd return to being friendless and living with her fosters in her miserable life of the past two years. Her eyes turned misty.

"Yeah. I have no idea what they look like."

"Seriously? You have no photographs? Not one?"

"None."

Hailey remembered seeing the picture frame and the fake photo on Minno's bedside table. Now she understood why. Even a phony mother and father were better than none at all.

"I'd give anything to hug my mother," Hailey said. Her words trailed off. The pain of her broken heart flooded her brain. She fought down erupting tears, reminding herself she would never cry again. Then she cried.

"You never told me what happened to your mother," Minno queried. She realized right after speaking that the words would rekindle painful memories Hailey probably wished to forget.

"She dropped me off at school one day. Never came back. I was eight. Been with fosters ever since. My own mother didn't want me."

When Hailey sobbed, Gutty brought her closer.

Ensconced in the thick of the undergrowth a few feet away, Dulfay shed a tear as he listened. The Palladins were sworn enemies, yet these two little girls had found a way under his skin and inside his heart.

"We're gonna need serious therapy when we get home," Hailey said loud enough for Minno to hear. Then Hailey turned over and finally fell into an exhausted sleep.

When Minno closed her eyes she imagined her mother's loving smile.

The morning sun brought biscuits from the Forbits and a spirited march out of the forest. Nole once again begged to be untied, so he might stretch his arms. Commander Dulfay only looked at him before proceeding to hasten his stride to take the lead ahead of the others.

Shortly after the sun reached its zenith, Commander Dulfay raised an arm, halting his rabbit clan mid-stride. The soldiers all dropped to a knee, hands on their swords.

Gutty and the girls wove through the rabbits to reach the front.

"Why we stopping?" Minno asked frustrated. Something Dulfay found most disconcerting. Grassy open fields stretched before them, beyond the grass rose an isolated soaring cliff. They couldn't have reached Antinarra.

The commander pointed to a cavern's black hollow near the top of the cliff.

"Antinarra," he said.

19

"No. No way. You're saying we ..." Hailey interjected, much to Minno's dismay.

"We have led you to your destination. We go no further," Dulfay added.

The words conveyed an ominous tone—one that sent chills through both Minno and Hailey. What was in that black hole that suddenly sent a foreboding tremor rippling through them? And why did the Forbit clan refuse to go any closer to this place? What was in Antinarra that would keep them at bay?

As they gazed off at the cliff, wondering how they might ever find a way up to the opening, the ground rumbled. The low resonant quaking grew more intense. Then crystal spears ripped from the ground at obtuse angles. The rabbits scattered.

"What is that?" Minno asked.

"Craveaux. More creatures have fallen. He grows stronger against us. Soon the Soma will come, we will all be saved."

"The Soma?" Gutty asked, surprised. How would the Forbit clan know about the Soma? Surely they would avoid a giant troll if it appeared before them.

"Yes, a giant, powerful Forbit to rescue us from the tyrant that hunts us all. Go now," Dulfay explained.

Gutty assumed the lead into the grassy field with Hailey at his side. They would soon reach their destination, and Minno would at last be with her parents. A proud smile swarmed Gutty's face. He, himself, had brought the girls to this point. Then sadness crept in. For the first time, he realized their journey together would soon end. They would part ways. He and Nole would return to the Forest of Perpetual Night to attempt to exact their revenge for what Craveaux had done to them.

Minno held back with the commander.

"Had we lost, what would you have done with the troll?" she asked.

"Set him free, of course," Dulfay said.

The commander found it strange she would pose such a question. Trolls and Forbits had been aligned against Palladins for three generations. While their alliance at best was tenuous, they both realized only by joining forces could they ever defeat their enemy. And until they destroyed Craveaux, they must tolerate each other, even though Forbits detested the smell of trolls. Trolls, conversely, had no disagreement with Forbits, only that they preferred to avoid them whenever possible.

"He's not our prisoner. He's our friend."

Dulfay looked at her confused. Palladins hunted trolls and Forbits for Craveaux's bounty. Most lived well from trapping them and taking advantage of their docile nature.

"What of Nole?" Minno pressed. She couldn't allow the Forbits to do anything bad to him. For all his faults, Nole had worked in earnest to help her along the way. She owed him for that.

On this, Dulfay thought. He could see in Minno's eyes that this Palladin meant something to her.

"He has brought us no harm. We are not the heartless creatures you might think us to be. You may keep him, though I cannot understand why. May fortune guide you on your journey," Dulfay said.

"Hey, Forbit, I don't suppose I could get a sword ..." Nole pressed while being unbound.

Dulfay just looked at him while the other rabbits bid their farewell and receded back into the forest. Nole jogged to catch up with the girls, flapping his arms like a bird in joyous freedom.

"My feet hurt. I'm tired," Hailey moaned as they trudged through chest-high grass. They had only been walking thirty minutes after leaving the rabbits behind when Gutty stopped.

He turned around, opening his mouth to speak. But nothing came out. At the fringe of the field, where the high grass yielded to forest trees, the stalks parted as something worked into the growth in their wake. He could make out three distinct movements. The Ooglys!

"They found us. We must go faster," he finally said.

"Can they catch us before we reach Auntie Narra?" Minno asked.

Gutty sized up the distance to the sheer cliff.

"Not if we run," he muttered, sprouting to his full nine-foot height in a second. He grabbed a girl in each arm before lumbering through the grass at a jogging pace.

Nole kicked into a run, muttering something about being swordless. In a few moments he reached Gutty.

A tightly-packed woodland of towering pine and spruce preceded the cliff. Once amongst the trees, the group zigzagged, trying to keep a pace that would prevent the Oogly brothers from reaching them before they arrived at the cliff. They hoped their chaotic pattern might confuse the Ooglys trying to lock onto their scent. They knew once the brothers locked onto them, there'd be no deviation until they had captured their prey.

Yet Minno had no inkling how they would scale such a near-vertical precipice in order to reach the safety of the black hollow.

Puffing, Gutty stumbled over the rough terrain, slowing to a stop.

"What's wrong?" Hailey asked.

She watched the path in their wake, certain at any second the Ooglys would appear, and they'd be captured, or worse, shot with an arrow.

Gutty's breathlessness kept him from speaking. Instead, he pointed.

"That's just great," Minno moaned in an exasperated, whining way.

"Like we haven't been through enough," Hailey called into the trees, hoping some cosmic force might offer up some aid.

They stared at a deep jagged ravine a dozen paces before them. A rickety one-man bridge provided the only way across. The ravine dove a hundred feet to churning white water cutting a path through it.

"That will never hold me," Gutty conceded.

"I know," Minno muttered.

"Looks rotted. Doubt it would even hold us," Hailey added.

Nole surveyed the landscape.

"You girls will be safe now. Antinarra's just over the bridge. Gutty, we need to go," Nole said. He watched for signs of the Ooglys. If they left now, they might escape before the Ooglys arrived.

Gutty said nothing.

"Look, if we split up, some of us have a chance. If the Ooglys come after us, the girls are in the clear. If the Ooglys go after the girls, we're ..." Nole stopped, his words began betraying his own argument.

"We stay together. There must be some way to cross," Gutty said.

"Sure," was all Nole could say. He returned to watching for the imminent Oogly brothers' arrival.

Minno attempted the bridge's first plank. It creaked in the agony of her weight. But it held. She offered an unconvincing thumbs-up.

Hailey shook her head. There were at least fifty more on the bridge. One plank did not make a crossing successful.

Minno straddled the second plank, slowly shifting weight onto it.

Crack! The plank split.

Minno screamed as she fell through.

Nole snared her hand! He yanked her back to safety.

They watched the splintered wood hit the water below.

"We're not leaving until Antinarra," Gutty stammered with no uncertainty in his voice. Nole knew from that tone challenging Gutty's decision would be useless.

"Fine. How do we cross then?" he responded, hoping that by mulling over the problem Gutty might see Nole's proposal as their only option.

Minno sized up the distance, looking down along the ravine to see if a shorter distance across existed. As expected, the foot bridge spanned the narrowest point.

"Jumping's not an option," Hailey cautioned, watching Minno's brain churning behind her eyes.

"I'm working on it." Minno pursed her lips in deep thought. There had to be a way across. But she had to find it quickly. She knew the Ooglys were closing in. They could travel along the ravine, hoping for another bridge or another span that might aid them.

Then she sized up a tall tree, one closest to the ravine's edge.

"Gutty, can you knock this tree down so it falls across the ravine to form a bridge?" she asked.

Gutty eyed the tree. He smiled. Wrapping his arms around the entire trunk was the easy part. Getting the roots to give way was an entirely different challenge. One he could only hope he could handle.

Gutty lined up behind the tree, calculated how he must push to force the trunk in the right direction, then heaved with all his strength.

Crack!

The roots weakened. The tree angled sixty degrees toward the ravine. There it stopped and crept back to near upright.

"Yeah! That's it, Gutty. You got it, big guy. Give it another one with all you've got," Hailey cheered.

"Work faster," Nole said, returning from the forest.

Gutty spit into his hands, flexed his biceps once more and drove his shoulder into the tree. With a grunt and groan that bellowed through the woodland, Gutty heaved again.

Roots snapped like rubber bands. The trunk yielded to forty-five degrees toward the ground. The earth at their feet erupted into large dirt clods.

Gutty screamed, pushed again.

The tree gave way completely. Gnarly roots surrendered to Gutty's force and released from the ground. The tree toppled over the ravine.

But the treetop fell just inches short of reaching the other side, and as such, the tree flipped head-over-heel into the ravine, plunging into the water below.

"What a plan," Nole muttered, shaking his head.

Watching the tree in the water, Minno felt a stiff breeze sweeping up the wall of the ravine across her face.

"We're out of time," Gutty said. He pointed into the forest. Something was moving downhill.

"Any other ideas?" Hailey asked.

"You didn't think of any," Minno snapped.

"Don't snap at me. I'm just trying to help."

"Well, you're not helping."

"Well, I'm not the one with the magic bag, am I?" Hailey countered.

Both girls smiled. Then they threw their arms around each other in a hug. Gutty joined them, though he had no idea why they should be so joyous all of a sudden.

"Hello, can we hold off on this whole hugging thing until we get to the other side?" Nole interjected.

"Nole, can you cross using the bridge?" Minno asked.

She also could see three silhouettes moving through the trees toward them. She calculated they had mere minutes remaining before the Ooglys were upon them.

"Look, I'm not leaving Gutty ..." Nole said.

"Trust me. I'll get Gutty across."

Minno's words brought disbelieving stares from Hailey and Gutty.

"Yeah, I think so. But what about ..." Nole offered.

"Go, now," Minno commanded. Removing her bag from her shoulder, she moved to Gutty's back.

A quarter mile from the ravine, Moogly sniffed as she wove back and forth through the trees. Doogly and Foogly trailed, relying on her sharper sense of smell to guide them.

"We're close now," Moogly muttered.

She stopped, looked up. Three silhouettes darted amongst the trees.

"I sees 'em," Foogly said, pointing to the clearing at the ravine.

"We got 'em now. Move it, brothers," Moogly commanded.

Foogly kicked harder, puffing as he came astride Moogly, who sped up when Doogly began to overtake them both. Doogly screamed a howl of success! The trees thinned and Gutty's hulking form came into view.

Crash!

Doogly's clopping feet somehow got entangled with Moogly's, spilling her to the ground, where she encountered Foogly's feet, toppling him along with her. All three tumbled in the soft dirt.

From where they lay, they watched as some strange triangular shape in reddish brown surged away from them.

As Nole teetered mid-span, using the rope as footholds rather than the planks, Gutty sailed off the edge. He wore Minno's bag stretched arm-to-arm, with the two girls clinging on his back.

"Please don't die, please don't die," he whimpered, as the huge mass plummeted toward the churning water.

Gutty screamed in sheer terror!

Then the bag expanded to thirty times its size, trapping the rising air beneath it. Gutty and the girls rose, parasailing past Nole as he watched them glide across the expanse. They all cheered their success.

But at that very same moment, the Oogly brothers reached the ravine, standing flabbergasted at the sight.

"We're gonna make it," Gutty chimed.

"Wa-hoo!" Hailey rang out.

But during the entire five seconds the three of them sailed airborne, Minno kept her eyes tightly shut—she couldn't breathe. It seemed like forever to cross the chasm. She didn't open her eyes until Gutty landed safely on the other side.

Once he stopped, he released the bag to return to its normal shape.

Minno's ashen face slowly returned its fleshy hue, and she slung her bag back over her shoulder.

Gutty raced to the footbridge to help Nole leap from the rope to safely land beside them. They were all safe.

But the Oogly brothers hadn't given up yet. On their side of the ravine, Moogly sized up the footbridge. Doogly tried the third plank in line on the bridge. It creaked and cracked under his tenuous weight.

"We're gonna get that bag," Doogly said, determined.

"Then you go first," Moogly instructed.

Foogly intervened. "You go. You the fattest. If it holds you, it'll hold us," he said to Moogly, smiling from the brilliance of his logic.

Moogly whacked his head as hard as she could.

"Who's holding the egg horn?" Foogly then said, eyeing Doogly.

"Yeah, that's right," Moogly agreed.

"Fine," Doogly said, swallowing hard. His hands shook while sweat trickled down his cheeks. Before advancing that first step onto the rickety bridge, he rubbed the egg horn, bringing it out to look at it. What if the egg horn wasn't lucky? he pondered before starting out.

Mimicking exactly what he had seen Nole doing a few minutes earlier, Doogly climbed onto the rope instead of using the rotted planks.

"Ah, bug nuggets! They're crossing," Minno said from the other side, more to herself, though Doogly heard her.

The Oogly brother broke a slight smile at her comments. They would get their bounty after all.

After a dozen of Doogly's steps, Moogly ventured onto the rope, easing one small step at a time. Lastly, as Doogly neared the midpoint of the bridge's twenty-foot span, Foogly climbed onto the bridge's rope.

However, the additional weight of a third person caused the bridge to wobble. But it held as all three Ooglys began their treacherous passage. Each step forward had to be measured and painstakingly slow. Doogly looked up—Minno and Hailey were waiting on the other side.

Their smiles stopped him dead in his tracks. Those were the most devious smiles he had ever witnessed. He knew in his heart they meant deep trouble for him and his brothers.

"What are you doing?" Doogly stammered. He clutched the overhead rope tighter. Forehead sweat trickled into his eyes. He shook his head to clear his vision. His heart thumped erratically. He dared not look down at the rushing water.

"Nothing. What are *you* doing?" Hailey replied with her most polite adolescent innocence.

The words forced Moogly and Foogly to gulp in concern.

"Right about now, you gotta be asking yourself: Is that egg horn really lucky?" Minno said. She delivered each word slowly and deliberately, so as to rattle the lead Oogly as much as possible.

It took Doogly a second to realize where this exchange was really going. The girls were planning something ... something very bad for the Ooglys.

"Back up," he commanded his brothers.

"She wouldn't dare," Moogly offered.

Foogly wasn't willing to take that chance. Being the closest to solid ground, he backtracked in a panic, leaping the final few feet to reach safety.

"Go ahead. I dares you!" he shouted across without thinking.

"You crazy? We're still on the bridge," Doogly spat back through gritted carious teeth.

"Oh, yeah. I takes back that dare," Foogly corrected.

At that moment Gutty took hold of the thick timber stakes securing the bridge into the ground. With a grunt, he lifted—the stakes came loose, causing the bridge to wobble and droop even further.

"Let's not act in haste, shall we? Run!" Doogly blurted. He reversed his position on the rope to slide back toward safety.

"Oh, not so tough now, are we?" Minno rattled.

"What's the matter, Ooglys, chicken?" Hailey sniped.

Doogly and Moogly's legs cranked as fast as they could under the precarious circumstances.

Gutty ripped the stakes clear out of the earth, felt the bridge tug against him as the rope lowered another few feet. He dug his heels deeper into the soft soil to keep from being pulled over the edge. But he held the stakes until the Oogly brothers were safely on the other side. Despite the grave danger, Gutty still refused to bring himself to harm the Ooglys. Delay them, yes, confound them, certainly; but harm them—he couldn't do it.

With the Ooglys shaking fists at him, Gutty released the stakes, allowing the footbridge to crumple like a fluttering snake into the water below.

"This isn't over yet, troll," Doogly yelled across the chasm.

"You're dead meat, Nole!" Foogly added, the veins in his neck bulging in anger.

Gutty waved good-bye, inciting the Oogly brothers even more as the four advanced into the surrounding forest.

"They will find a way across," Gutty said, glancing back to see the Ooglys dash off along the ridge heading south.

"Let's be long gone by then," Nole said.

20

The four maintained a spirited pace, knowing now that Antinarra lie just ahead and the Ooglys, for the time being, were stranded far behind, sidetracked by the need to find a way across the ravine.

Minno couldn't help but think about her parents. What would they be like? Would they even recognize her? Of course, they wouldn't. She was a baby when they were separated. Wait a minute, grandpa never told her how they had become separated in the first place. For all her life she believed they were dead. Now they weren't, yet she never learned how they came to be apart. And how did they live in this world, while she lived in California with her grandpa. Was he even her real grandpa? Could that have been a lie also?

She shed all her fears when, through the opening in the trees, she glimpsed the high cliff ahead and the cavern opening. Her father would be there. He would protect her and Hailey. Nothing bad could happen to them once they reached Antinarra.

While Gutty walked ahead of the girls, he removed his egg horn and ran his fingers over the hard ivory curve.

"See an egg horn, pick it up ..." he said with the rhythm of a rhyme.

"'til the next new moon you'll have good luck," Minno added, coming up beside him, surprising herself when she blurted it out from her memory. A memory she never even knew she had.

"Yeah, right," Nole offered with skepticism clinging to his voice.

"Okay, so how did you know that?" Hailey put in, "that come from your grandpa's book?"

"It must have. I don't know how else I would have known it."

"How long has he been reading it to you?"

"As long as I can remember."

Gutty stopped and laid the egg horn across his palm so the girls could see it. When Hailey touched it—the tip pricked her finger, causing her to recoil. She sucked her finger to stop the trickle of blood.

"Cool. So why's an egg horn lucky?" she asked after taking her finger out to see that the bleeding had stopped.

"Dragons need them to break through the shell. A few days after hatching, it falls off," Gutty explained.

"Yeah, so why's it lucky?" Hailey persisted.

Gutty looked at her as if he didn't understand.

"It just is," he added when he could think of no other explanation.

"Superstitious hooey, that's what that is. There's no such thing as good luck, or bad luck, for that matter," Hailey said.

"Says you," Gutty countered.

"Mmm-hmm. S-e-z me," Hailey shot right back, sounding like a brat.

Minno smiled. Hailey was actually disputing the existence of luck—with a troll! If trolls are real and dragons are real and flowers that can make music are real, why then couldn't luck be real? Certainly luck had accompanied them this far on their journey.

"What?" Hailey said, when Minno just looked at her.

Gutty tucked his egg horn away, picked Hailey up to place her on his shoulder as his way of agreeing to disagree. Only the arrival of the next new moon would determine whose beliefs were right, and whose were wrong.

After another hour's walk, the trees thinned. They came upon an open field preceding the base of the sheer precipice. The black hollow looked even higher up the cliff now, and they could tell from the smooth rock face that climbing it would be near impossible.

Between them and the cliff sat a huge field of Patsche, mushroom-like plants, whose caps were all covered with hair. Not just hair, but groomed hair, ranging from the vibrant red of strawberries to the blackest black of a crow's wing. They arrived to survey a sea of buzz cuts, spikes, Mohawks and curly bushes undulating before them.

"Any ideas how we're getting up there?" Hailey asked as Gutty lumbered along. Even standing atop Gutty's shoulders would fall far short of reaching the opening. She tightened her grip on Gutty's neck hair as they breached the Patsche field.

With each step deeper into the Patsche, the plants grew a matter of inches, as if they were acting to thwart their advance. After a dozen steps, the Patsche were knee high and so dense that walking became difficult.

"You seeing this?" Minno asked.

"Mushrooms ... yuck. Should we stop?" Hailey replied.

"We're so close now. I'm not stopping for ..." Minno picked her way more carefully through the dirty white plants with deep brown gill-like structures on the undersides of their caps.

"For what?" a voice chimed in with a distinctly British accent.

"What did you say?" Minno asked, turning to see where the words came from.

"I didn't say a thing," Hailey offered quickly. But she had heard it also.

"You say something?" she asked of Gutty.

"I don't think I did."

"It wasn't me," Nole added, even though no one asked him. He felt slighted that neither girl asked him, though they asked Gutty.

The Patsche surrounding them now stood waist high. And they seemed to be swaying, though the surrounding air was still. They kept bumping Minno as she tried to advance toward the cliff.

"Anyone else concerned about the size of these mushrooms?" Hailey asked. She was glad to be on Gutty's shoulder. For Gutty, each step further into the field became harder and harder to complete.

"We are the Patsche Collective," another voice said. This one had the tone of royalty. With those words, all the Patsche popped up and animated in unison.

"United we grow, huzzah!" they chimed together.

"I would turn around, if I were you," the Patsche beside Minno said.

It appeared as if the gill-like structures on the underside of their caps were generating the words.

"Which one of you said that?" Minno asked.

"I don't see how we can scale that cliff without hand holds," Gutty offered.

The strange creatures had grown so large, and now so dense, that Minno, Gutty and Nole could move no further into the Patsche field. Nole lingered at the rear, having an especially difficult time making his way through the plants.

"Maybe you can whip up an escalator with that bag of yours?" Hailey asked.

"She has the dragon wing!" a female voice rang out.

"Hello, maybe we shouldn't be talking about the b-a-g right now," Minno said. Her eyes fired daggers at Hailey.

"Right. They can talk, but you're thinking they can't spell. Sorry, I didn't realize we were keeping that a secret from the mushrooms," Hailey said.

"Well, now you do," Minno snapped back.

"Yeah, well, it's too late for these mushroom things," Hailey persisted.

"No. That can't be. Only the great Soma will have the dragon wing," yet another Patsche voice joined in. This one spoke with a distinctly cockney accent.

"We all know the great Soma is a giant and powerful Patsche ... the true leader of the Patsche Collective! He will save us from the tyrant of the valley," the regal Patsche offered.

"United we grow, huzzah!" they all chimed again, as if on cue.

"Are you sure it's the dragon wing?" a different female Patsche asked, this one much older than the previous one.

"She's too scrawny to be a Soma," a gruff-voiced Patsche added.

Finding herself trapped in the field of Patsche so thick now that she couldn't force her foot ahead to take another step, Minno unshouldered her bag. She opened it in the most menacing way she could.

"Don't make me use this ... this bag on you, Patsches ... collections. Cuz you r-e-e-a-l-l-y won't like that!" she said with the meanest, toughest voice she could muster. Then she realized the absurdity of her statement. Was she seriously hoping to frighten mushrooms with a handbag?

All the Patsche shivered in unison.

"Oh, yeah, we're s-o-o-o scared," a Patsche said.

"Oh, look, I think I soiled myself," another whimpered.

"All right, listen up, you freaky mushrooms. We have a great big troll here! And he's r-e-e-e-a-l-l-y ferocious!" Hailey said, losing her patience with the plants. She paused for effect. "And he eats mushrooms, I mean Patsches for breakfast!"

Gutty groaned uncomfortably.

"So just watch it," she concluded, hoping she could frighten them. It was only after she said it that she realized she should have threatened to put them on a pizza if they didn't behave. Of course, did these things even know what a pizza was?

All the Patsche laughed in unison. As they did, their gill-like structures oscillated back and forth in wave-like motions.

Nole just shook his head, choosing to remain silent. He knew the Patsche hated Palladins—actually, every creature in the land hated the Palladins, so there would be little chance of making friends with these creatures.

"We're not Palladins, if that's what you think. We seek Auntie Narra," Minno said.

"Really? Good show, you're at the right place then," another Patsche offered.

"Why did you tell her that? How do you know they can be trusted," a female Patsche said.

"Hel-lo ... dragon wing," the first Patsche replied.

"Why on earth do you have a filthy, disgusting troll?" a new female Patsche chimed in.

Minno vacillated back and forth, looking for the one who had spoken. She couldn't tell.

"He's not disgusting," Minno shot in. "Okay, maybe dirty, and he does smell, granted, but that's from traveling. He's our friend. He helped us get here. He's sweet and gentle. We mean no harm."

"*He's our friend,*" another Patsche mocked. "Trolls have no friends."

"Please, tell us how we reach Auntie Narra. It's very important," Minno pressed.

"Just walk up the cliff. If you truly have the dragon wing, you will not fall. But if you're trying to trick us ..." the gruff Patsche said.

"What if *they're* trying to trick *us*? What if they're going to trap us and eat us?" Hailey ventured.

The Patsche responded with laughter.

"Eat Palladins, disgusting!" a Patsche said.

"Besides, we ate three hours ago, my dear," a high-pitched female Patsche said.

"I say, I'm watching what I eat these days. Look at me from the side, do I look like I've put on weight?" came from another. The Patsche next to Minno leaned into her and to the side to reveal a gut-like bump in the middle of its stalk.

"No, no. Not one bit. You look smashing!"

"Bah, I'm standing beside a troll. Everyone looks great next to one of them."

"Just walk up the cliff, huh? Okay, sure. And how do we do that?" Minno asked, hoping one of them might slip and reveal something that would help them.

She started forward again. As she did, the Patsche spurted taller by a few inches. At that moment, Nole grabbed her elbow.

"We climb onto them," he whispered.

"Hel-lo, we're surrounded by these things. I think they can hear you even if you whisper," Hailey said.

That got her an angry look from Nole.

"What? They can't hold my weight," Gutty pointed out.

"That's right, fatty! I'd go on a diet if I were you. Just go back the way you came," a male Patsche said.

"Hey, let's not get personal here. Just because someone, who shall remain nameless, likes to snack a little too much . . ." Hailey said.

"It'll work, trust me," Nole forced in to cut Hailey off.

"He's been right so far," Hailey agreed.

"No, he hasn't," Minno countered.

Hailey gave Gutty a playful light slap on the back.

"Onward and upward, fatty! Just kidding, Gutty."

"Uh, huh. You go ahead," Gutty said, setting Hailey down into the Patsche Collective.

Nole ventured first onto a Patsche. Once he stabilized himself on the cap, he motioned to Minno. She pulled herself onto the Patsche in front of her then steadied herself on the way to standing up.

Then Hailey climbed onto another.

The row of Patsche now standing between them and the cliff grew a little taller, as if trying to block them from advancing. But in so doing, they had inadvertently formed the beginnings of a stairway.

"Yeah! It's totally working," Minno chimed.

The girls leapt from their Patsches to the next higher Patsches. Ahead of them, another row of Patsche rose up to form another stair. So the girls and Nole jumped to that stair.

But Gutty still refused to move.

"Come on, Gutty. It will work," Minno called back.

"It won't," Gutty insisted.

Back at the base, the first rows of Patsche shrank back to a few inches high, in effect erasing the staircase. The higher the girls and Nole climbed, the greater the distance grew between them and the ground. Leaving them without a way back down.

At twenty feet off the ground, Nole stopped. He looked back. He didn't like what he saw.

"You better come right now!" he said.

Gutty turned to check out what Nole had seen.

The Ooglys exited the forest and were dashing into the field.

Gutty leapt onto the first row of Patsche, fully expecting to crush them with his burgeoning mass. They wobbled—but they held his weight.

"What did you eat for lunch, boulders?" one said under the strain of Gutty's mass.

Gutty hopped like a Forbit to reach the next row. He jumped quickly upward until he was three rows behind the girls as they climbed as fast as they could. Nole held back, waiting for Gutty to catch up.

"We're going to have to move faster," Nole said, hoping to spur Gutty on.

"This is as fast as I can move without losing my balance."

The girls could see the black hollow of the cavern a few feet above their heads. But then Minno made a critical mistake—she looked down. Her stomach erupted into her throat. Her hands and her knees suddenly weakened. When she looked out, the Oogly brothers were sprinting faster.

"Go, Minno. C'mon, Gutty, you're a graceful ballerina! You can do this," Hailey cheered.

The girls were only two rows of growing Patsche from the ledge leading to the cave. They scaled more desperately as the Patsche continued to create the path for them.

"Graceful ballerina, right," Gutty said, huffing and puffing.

At the ledge, Hailey held on tight and lowered a hand to assist Minno up and over to the cave entrance. It seemed only right that she should be the first to see her parents.

Minno crawled over the side, sprawled out on the cool rock ledge and stared up at cottony clouds drifting lazily across the sky.

She made it! She was here.

Hailey came over the ridge behind her, sprawling out next to her. Their labored breathing was the only sound in the air. They clasped hands.

"We're here!" Minno said. Her smile totally consumed her face.

"This better be the right place, cuz there's no turning back now," Hailey said.

Gutty's hand came over the edge and held there. The huge troll struggled to gain a hold with his other hand.

Arrows whizzed by.

Nole, who was still behind Gutty, and therefore still in the line of fire from the Ooglys below, hugged the cliff face.

The Patsches bowed outward away from the cliff to act as a barrier and deflect the arrows, which fell back to the ground, causing the Oogly brothers to scatter.

"Help me, please. I ... can't ... make ..." Gutty expelled between gasps.

Gutty's hand slipped! He dropped, dangling by the other hand.

Minno quickly cast her bag over the ledge for him to latch onto.

"Grab it!"

Gutty threw an arm up in time to grasp the bag.

With Gutty's massive weight, Minno should have been pulled off the side of the cliff; instead the bag stretched while Minno slid forward a few feet.

"Hailey, help."

Hailey slid in behind Minno, wrapping her arms around her friend's waist. Both girls dug their heels in. With grunting and groaning, Gutty's hand came over the ledge, followed by his head. He crested the ledge and lay gasping. The girls toppled beside him, too exhausted to speak.

Nole's hand came over next.

"Some help here," he begged.

Minno crawled back to the edge, where she pulled Nole up onto the landing.

"You think anybody in Blue Lake's gonna believe we hauled a nine-foot troll over this ledge?" Minno asked rhetorically.

"Oh, yeah, my summer vacation, by Minno and Hailey," Hailey replied.

"I'm a beautiful ballerina?" Gutty gasped.

Minno returned to her feet first, dusted herself off and slung her bag over her shoulder. She high-fived Hailey, who in turn hugged Gutty.

"You rock, fatty!" Hailey giggled.

"I can't believe it. We've reached Auntie Narra," Minno said.

The four stared into the lightless chasm. Minno knew she had to be the first to enter, though none of them knew what to expect once they breached the darkness.

21

Sunlight penetrated no further than a dozen paces into the hollow on the side of the cliff. The air carried the strangest pungent odor, not one Minno or Hailey had experienced before this moment.

The cavern ceiling loomed thirty feet above them and nothing moved but them once they were inside. As the light degraded into darkness, they stopped. Uncertainty and fear swam inside their heads. How could this place be Antinarra? Where were they? Was this a trap?

"This isn't good. We should back out and leave, Gutty," Nole said.

Of course, Nole had no idea where they might go—certainly not back down the cliff where the Ooglys waited. They had no idea how to ascend the cliff to reach the top. For the moment, their only course was the darkness ahead.

"Hello. Anybody home?" Minno ventured, her soft voice failing to carry very far.

Nole retreated for the tenuous safety of the light.

"Why do you come here?" a gravelish voice rose from within the bowels of this place.

"We're looking for Auntie Narra," Minno offered, trying to sound optimistic. She had no idea how they might be received by the voice.

Two strange yellow eyes floated out of the darkness. They seemed far enough away so as to not elicit fear at the moment. Minno could tell they were human pupils.

"It's An-ti-nar-ra. Not Auntie Narra. Advance no further," the voice commanded in a menacing tone. Minno suspected it was a female's voice.

"How do I even know you are Antinarra?" Minno asked.

Fire whooshed out of the darkness, evaporating well short of reaching them.

Nole cowered further behind the girls.

"I think we should say nothing to anger this Antinarra," Gutty offered, his words cracking with fear.

A yellow glow swarmed over a beautiful woman's face perched a few feet taller than the girls. Minno's heart warmed at the sight. Antinarra wasn't a place—it was a woman. Someone Grandpa Esri must have trusted enough to send Minno to her.

"I come . . ." Minno started with relief in her voice.

Nole, however, upon seeing the exquisite face, advanced to the forefront, smoothing jostled hair and straightening his clothes as best he could. He couldn't take his eyes off the woman's wonderful beauty. He even detected a smile as she studied him.

"Here, let me. My lady, you are the most beautiful creature I have ever seen," Nole started.

"Flattery will serve you nil in this place, Palladin," Antinarra responded. The sharpness of her words revealed her disdain for Palladins. As a result, Nole felt in grave danger. Something was wrong here. Something Nole rifled through his brain to try to uncover.

"We, I mean, me and my troll friend here, ah, seek only to reunite this child with her parents. See, I stand before you unarmed," Nole explained, raising his arms to show he levied no sword.

"A noble Palladin. Ha!" Antinarra responded.

Nole's eyelids fluttered. The rush of unwanted sleep spread through his brain. His legs weakened. He had only a single second before ...

"Not now," Nole muttered as he crumpled to the cavern floor sound asleep.

Seeing him helpless, Antinarra advanced into the yellow light. A dragon's body had been seamlessly grafted onto the trunk of a beautiful woman. From the waist up, Antinarra was completely human. Below were green scales, a long sweeping tail and four clawed feet.

"What happened to him?" she asked.

"He does that. One of Craveaux's spells," Minno offered.

"How is Desrilian?" Antinarra asked.

"My grampa's name is Esri. Is that who you mean?"

In the darkness Minno's irises had turned to silver.

"Yes, it would be. Come forward, Minnovera, so I might see you better." Antinarra could hardly conceal her surprise. "Your parents will be so proud."

Minno and Hailey remained steadfast, too frightened to even move at the sight of this person, or rather half person, before them. Yet Antinarra's voice melted the fears the girls sought to conceal in her presence.

"You know me? You know my parents? You can help us!" Minno said with vaulting jubilation.

Goose flesh rose under the hair on Gutty's arms. He had succeeded. For once in his life he had done something right. They were in the place they needed to be.

"I am Antinarra. Come," she said. As she turned, her tail swished, forcing Gutty to duck. He scooped Nole into his arms before following the girls, who walked beside Antinarra.

Leading them deeper into the descending cavern, Antinarra's yellow glow illuminated the path. After a dozen direction changes, neither Minno nor Hailey felt confident they could find their way back to the entrance.

"Do we trust her? She's half dragon. They eat people," Gutty risked when it seemed like she might be leading them to a slaughter.

"Nonsense, we only eat rude trolls," Antinarra said without looking back.

Gutty gulped his fear.

"Actually ... I'm not a troll ... exactly. I'm a beautiful ballerina," Gutty replied, hoping to diffuse the anger he might have stirred up.

"Whatever," Antinarra replied. She led them into a vaulted cavern with a shimmering lighted lake in its center. Swarms of glowing fish darted about under the clear water, following the girls as they skirted the perimeter.

Without warning, a twenty-foot dragon lurched out from a black alcove, spraying fire over the water.

"Wait! They're not Palladins," Antinarra shouted.

The dragon's head coiled. It came to rest eye-to-eye with Minno. The dragon's eyes had the exact same silver-colored irises. For Minno it was like looking into a mirror as her eyes held the dragon's.

Minno and Hailey froze, too terrified to even breathe, let alone make their legs move. But in that moment, with Minno eye-to-eye with the monster, she realized their eyes were identical.

"Please don't eat us," Hailey cried, her knees audibly rattling in fear.

Gutty dared not budge for fear the dragon might shift to him and Nole.

Instead, the dragon laughed.

"She has your eyes," Antinarra said softly.

"She does," the dragon said with a voice so warm and gentle that both girls shed their concern.

"I'm trying to find my parents," Minno offered.

Neither broke eye contact.

"You have," the dragon said. Glistening tears formed in the creature's eyes.

Hailey and Minno exchanged a look of unfathomable disbelief. She didn't know what to think, or how to feel. This was not what Minno expected their reunion to be.

The dragon shifted to scrutinize Nole asleep in Gutty's arms.

"He helped us find you," Minno quickly offered.

"Appears he's sleeping," Antinarra said.

"Craveaux's spell," Gutty offered.

"B-but ... I ... m-my grampa," Minno stuttered, searching for words to express the wild notions whipping around in her brain.

The dragon returned to Minno.

"Desrilian was supposed to tell you all you needed to know."

"How can this ... I mean ... this can't be. It's impossible," Minno said, realizing this could never be understood.

"My mother's name is Sachea," Minno said at the exact moment the dragon also said, "I am Sachea."

Minno stared.

"Minnovera, in Ambrosia all is possible," Sachea added.

"But grampa said you're in grave danger. I had to rescue you."

"We are. Craveaux has captured your father, along with most of our kind. We can no longer fight the Palladins ourselves. I fear soon his soldiers will find us."

"We were expecting only you," Antinarra said.

"Yeah. Long story. Not really. Hailey, she's my friend here, she got sucked into the portal. She was sleeping over when that thing attacked."

"I sent messengers through to warn Esri. One of them must have succeeded," Antinarra said.

"No, no, this can't be. You're not my mother. You can't be."

A sad tear formed in Sachea's eye. She blinked it out to roll down her shimmering green scaly cheek.

"I know this is difficult for you," Sachea said.

"How can I be your child?"

"Come. I suspect you and Hailey must be hungry and tired, and in need of many answers. We both have many questions."

"What about Nole and Gutty?" Minno asked.

"They have brought you safely to me. For that, I am in their debt, even if one's a troll and the other's a Palladin. No harm will come to them from us. I promise you that."

"But they do smell," Antinarra added.

"Yeah, tell me about it," Hailey agreed.

22

The Oogly brothers surrounded their small fire, chomping on stale crumbling biscuits, staring blankly into the dancing yellow flickers.

"Craveaux will find out if we get our hands on the bag," Doogly said.

"Not if we don't tells him," Foogly said.

"He will. Craveaux knows everything that goes on in this land."

"There may be a way even the great Craveaux will not find out," Moogly said, hypnotized by the flames.

Behind them, ensconced in the black night, the green eyes hovered. When Doogly turned to look in the direction of the eyes, they closed and disappeared. When he turned back to the fire, they reappeared as if a pair of eyelids had come down then came back up.

"I say we wait. They have to come down," Moogly offered. She watched her brothers' eyes. Neither revealed their thoughts with their face. For a moment she wondered if she could even trust her own blood with such a powerful prize. Perhaps if she were to get her hands on the bag, they would take it from her.

"There must a way to force those Patsche into helping us reach the cavern. We're so close now, brothers," Foogly said.

"They will never help us," Moogly said, "We're on our own from here on out."

"What if we offer them something to eat?" Doogly offered.

"Oh, yeah. That's good. You know what Patsche eat?" Moogly asked.

"What?" Foogly seemed genuinely dumbfounded.

"You don't want to know," Moogly said.

23

Sachea and Antinarra sat around a fire across from the girls while Hailey licked her fingers, savoring every last taste of what Antinarra had prepared for them. For the first time since coming through the portal, the girls felt full and content.

"I haven't eaten this good since we came here," Hailey offered. She wished there would have been more to eat, but felt it impolite to ask for more. She noticed Minno had only eaten half her dinner and for a fleeting moment considered snatching some of hers. But then she thought better.

"When Desrilian foresaw our future, he knew we had to a find a way to stop Craveaux. So your father and I agreed to take human form to bring you into the world. Your grandfather volunteered to remain human to keep you safe until ..."

"What did grampa see?" Minno asked.

"Our extinction," Sachea answered with great sadness in her voice.

"How, why?"

"For a hundred years the dragons ruled the skies, while the Palladins ruled the valleys. All creatures lived in peace throughout the land. Then war broke out amongst the Palladins," Sachea said.

"Craveaux believed that all power should go to the Palladins, and all creatures must pledge their servitude to them," Antinarra added.

"So he started the war?" Hailey asked.

"Craveaux came to Desrilian with a guarantee that no dragon would be harmed if all dragons rallied to unseat King Jess-Kenoe from power."

"Did the dragons fight?" Minno asked.

"I was just getting to that," Antinarra said. "The dragons helped Craveaux defeat the king and force him into exile."

"So why does Craveaux hunt the dragons now?"

"In his victory, Craveaux came to understand the great power that magic held in this land," Antinarra said.

"Palladins have no magic. They are weak, frail creatures," Sachea said.

"Craveaux used the dragons to seize the throne and the fortress. Then he set out to find a way to steal our magic. When we became aware of creatures being captured and brought to the fortress for a bounty, we knew Craveaux had found what he desired."

"When did this start?" Minno asked.

"Eighteen years ago. We have opposed Craveaux's army since then. He lied to us and used us to gain power. Now he knows if he can steal our magic, no creature in the land can oppose him."

"But they say you eat people, even children," Minno interrupted.

Sachea laughed.

"A myth perpetuated by the Palladins to use against us. We never sought to destroy them until they came to destroy us. Craveaux's rise to power brought death and fear to all in Ambrosia."

"How do we stop him? He commands an army. We've seen it," Minno said.

"We seek only to prevent our own extinction in his evil hands," Sachea said.

"But he is only one man, and so much smaller than you. Surely the trolls and dragons can unite to fight them," Hailey said.

Her words brought frowns to both Sachea and Antinarra. There was much Minno had yet to understand about her new land.

"The magic he steals from us gives him great powers. Our numbers are few now. Soon we will be unable to stop him."

"How many dragons remain free?"

"There are five of us left scattered throughout the kingdom. Your father has helped us stay one step ahead of Craveaux's hunters. Then he himself was taken," Sachea said. Sadness weighted her words. Tears clouded her eyes at the thought of losing him.

"Is he?"

"We can only hope you have arrived in time," Antinarra said, when Sachea found it impossible to speak.

"Does Craveaux ever leave his fortress?"

"His fortress is what keeps him safe from all of us. That is why we need your help," Sachea said.

"But what am I supposed to do? I'm only thirteen. How could I possibly help you?"

"Craveaux covets dragon magic the most. It is the most powerful magic in the land. Without it, Palladins are useless, like that one sleeping in the cavern away from us."

"Together we can become strong again," Antinarra burst in. She could contain her excitement no longer. What they had been hoping for, for so long, had come to pass. Of course, it wasn't exactly what they expected, but Minno could serve them well.

"Can't you become human again? And be my parents like you were when I was born?" Minno asked.

"I'm sorry. Your father and I surrendered our magic to have you. We are both vulnerable now. If Craveaux knew what we had done, he would surely hire every dragon hunter in the land to destroy us and to destroy you."

"Why?"

"Because it is written a Soma will someday return to this land to destroy the evil that lurks on high," Antinarra said.

"Where is my father?"

"We believe he's in Craveaux's dungeon," Antinarra said.

"Should Craveaux learn that Osomoray has no magic in him, he will surely kill him," Sachea said.

"We must find a way to free him along with the others," Minno said. "But what about grampa?" she added, thinking about what she might do.

"Your grandfather excised his dragon wings to preserve his magic for you. That bag you carry is one of Desrilian's wings. It is very potent in your hands. Never let them get it. If Craveaux obtained that bag, he would become powerful enough to destroy any in Ambrosia who dared to oppose him."

"I won't, I promise. This is all I have of him. I'm afraid the monster that attacked us got grampa after I came through the portal. I won't know if he survived until we return home."

"We are vulnerable, so we hide, waiting for your arrival," Sachea said.

"How long have you been hiding?" Hailey asked.

"Thirteen years," Antinarra answered.

"Tell us how we help," Minno said.

"You must infiltrate Craveaux's fortress, locate the dragons, and find a way to free them. Once free, we can command the skies once more and force Craveaux out of his stronghold," Sachea said.

"Yeah, about that. We've been to Craveaux's fortress. We didn't like what was going on so we left," Minno said.

"We've witnessed what Craveaux does to the creatures he imprisons. It's not pretty," Hailey added.

"Then you will change our destiny ..." Sachea began.

She stopped abruptly, peering deep into the dark tunnel leading to their chamber. Sachea looked to Antinarra.

The green eyes hovered in the darkness, observing their every move.

"Craveaux has found us," Sachea said, as if all life had been sucked out of her.

Minno turned to see the green eyes staring directly at her. She jumped up, threw open her bag, which she swung overhead to create a thick rolling dust cloud. In a few moments the cloud overtook the eyes, forcing them to close and disappear.

24

Craveaux catapulted from his chair, screaming while covering his bandaged eye sockets. Upon hearing the commotion, Sickly rushed in, followed by three other sycophants.

"What is it, high minister?" Sickly asked.

"Dragons!" Craveaux growled.

The sycophants cowered where they stood, casting their eyes every which way in terror. Sickly knew better. He immediately dropped to the floor.

Craveaux fired a random blue lightning bolt from his right hand. The sycophants hit the floor, covering their heads. The bolt ricocheted off the quartz walls and ceiling with a fierce sizzle.

The high minister rubbed his eye sockets. Then he began laughing maniacally, while his sycophants and Sickly returned to their feet.

"Too late. They have led Craveaux to you," the high minister said aloud, but speaking to himself. "Summon General Furion. The final dragons are within reach."

"Yes, high minister," Sickly said with as much enthusiasm as he could muster.

"Now leave!" Craveaux shouted.

The sycophants tripped over each other trying to get out.

Craveaux's smile grew large and ominous. Soon there would be no dragons left to oppose him. Then he would move forward with his plan.

25

Minno moved closer to Sachea. A familial bond locking them together had quickly formed, though Minno couldn't understand why. Was there something innate between them that she didn't realize existed before this? Some genetic link she never knew she had? Or did she feel a kinship to this dragon simply because she was told it was her mother? A part of Minno still refused to believe she could possibly be the offspring of two dragons. And if it were indeed true, why didn't she have any magical powers?

"Will Craveaux come after you?" she asked.

"Craveaux is only safe within his crystal walls. He cannot leave, or he becomes vulnerable."

"But Craveaux's soldiers will come," Antinarra said.

"I'm not going to let them harm you," Minno said.

She tightened her hand on her bag, realizing its magic would be what could protect her mother rather than her or Hailey.

"That is not your destiny, my child. He will send his soldiers, of that I am certain. But in so doing, he leaves himself exposed to you. My life and your father's life are expendable. You *must* save the others," Sachea said.

"I cannot . . ." Minno started.

But Sachea silenced her with her tears.

"She is too young to succeed," Antinarra said.

Both Sachea and Antinarra thought that very thought, but neither wanted to face it. After all, she was all they had. And time was running out for the dragons.

"Will you be safe here, mother?" Minno asked. She had called her mother. It felt strangely natural. She never thought she would ever call another mother.

Minno unconsciously placed her bag over her shoulder. She would do whatever it took to free her father and the others.

Sachea had no answer.

Gutty sat beside Nole in a dank, dimly lit cavern. Like seconds ticking away, water drops plopped from the ceiling at regular intervals.

"Where are we?" Nole yelled out, bolting upright.

"We are safe," was all Gutty offered.

"Wait a minute. Where is the beautiful woman I saw? Was she real?"

Nole sprang to his feet. Straightening his rumpled clothes, he marched out of the cavern.

"Wait! There is much you should know before ..." Gutty said, struggling to catch up. "This is not good."

Nole marched through the tall tunnels and turned to his right at a crossing tunnel emitting flickering light. A few minutes later, he entered the main cavern with Gutty behind him.

Sachea coiled, hissing and preparing to strike Nole down where he stood. Her sudden vicious movement froze Nole in his tracks. But the troll hunter's eyes were fixed on Antinarra.

"Mother!" Minno shouted to stop her before she might strike Nole dead.

Sachea backed away, albeit reluctantly.

"Mother? You called her mother? You said, mother," Nole stammered. Had he heard that correctly? That didn't make sense.

"He's still a Palladin," Sachea said.

"Be still, Palladin, there is much you need to know," Antinarra injected.

Nole's eyes widened with disbelief at seeing Antinarra's full form.

"You're," Nole stammered.

"Yes, I am," Antinarra replied as matter-of-factly as she could.

"I have heard the tales, but I . . ." Nole countered.

"Now you know the truth," Antinarra said.

"Tell us, Palladin, how we may breach Craveaux's fortress undetected," Sachea issued more like an order than a question.

Nole couldn't draw his eyes off Antinarra. Sachea's face turned stern when he failed to provide an immediate answer.

"There's an underground passage into the fortress from the Barrens. Few soldiers guard there," Nole offered.

"How can we trust him?" Antinarra said. Her eyes narrowed.

"I trust him," Minno cut in.

"You two can't go there. It is too dangerous," Gutty warned.

"I must. My father's life depends on it," Minno replied.

"No. We must. We're in this together," Hailey added.

"Don't tell me. Your father's a dragon also," Nole said.

"I will see you safely there," Gutty rose up to offer.

Nole's head turned with a jarring snap. For a long moment Gutty looked at Nole and got no response. But Gutty knew exactly what Nole was thinking.

"This is not our fight," Nole said.

"It is our fight. We said we would make Craveaux pay for what he has done to us," Gutty corrected.

"I cannot align with the dragons," Nole countered.

"Then we align with Minno," Gutty shot back.

"You will not be safe, Gutty. Craveaux will never let you slip through his hands again," Hailey said.

"We will not be fighting alone against him this time," Gutty said with a finality that Nole knew could not be challenged.

"Fine. We get you safely into the fortress. Then we're gone. We do this right, and Craveaux never finds out we betrayed him again," Nole said.

Antinarra led the girls to a chamber not far from the water, where inside, furry pelts lined the floor.

"Sleep now, the hour is late and on the morrow your journey to the fortress must begin," Antinarra said. Her voice revealed her uncertainty toward Minno's task.

"I will succeed," Minno said in her effort to calm Antinarra's concerns. "I must. Grampa Esri taught me enough."

Antinarra said nothing; rather she secured a torch to a crevasse in the side wall of the chamber and departed.

By the time Minno curled up in the corner with her pelt, Hailey had already fallen fast asleep. Sheer exhaustion had taken over her friend. The rest and nourishment they received would prepare them for what lie ahead. But there was nothing that could prepare their minds for what they were about to face.

An avalanche of sleep overtook Minno. And in her slumber she dreamt not of her mother or her father, but rather of her grandpa. In her mind's eye, she saw his arm fighting off the hairy-clawed appendage that grabbed him while he remained outside the portal. Through the blue light she witnessed the terror in Esri's eyes. Like a videotape, her mind fast forwarded, beyond what she actually witnessed as she disappeared into the portal. She watched Esri fend off the beast by jabbing a tree branch into the creature's single glaring red eye. When the beast released its grip to remove the object, Esri escaped.

The terror of the dream jolted Minno awake. She sprang upright, staring into flickering light from the dying torch. How long had she been asleep? Was it now day beyond the cavern?

More importantly, was her mind trying to tell her that her grandpa could have really escaped the monster? Or was it just her brain wishing he had, in order to avoid dealing with the heartache of losing the only family she knew for certain she had.

Then Minno lurched to her feet in panic. Her bag was gone! She searched the pelts from end to end. She realized at that moment Hailey was also gone.

"Hailey," she called out, suddenly terrified for her friend. They were supposed to be safe here. Her mother was supposed to protect them. What happened?

Minno bolted from the chamber in search of her friend. She followed the tunnel toward the faint glow of moonlight entering the caverns through the entrance. Then she saw Hailey in silhouette trudging slowly toward the light.

"Hailey."

But her friend refused to come about to acknowledge Minno's call.

Minno broke into a run. Hailey had her bag! She was dragging it along the ground as she approached the entrance on the cliff.

Hailey left the darkness of the cave to emerge into the shimmering moonlight. Her eyes only half open—she had no idea what she was doing, only that something compelled her to take the bag and walk to the edge of the ledge. She stopped when she felt cool night air sweeping up her face.

Raise your arm now, Craveaux's voice inside her brain commanded.

At first she resisted.

"Hailey, no," came from behind her.

Her hand came up with the bag in tow. She stared at the bag perplexed.

Extend your arm, then drop the bag over the cliff, that voice ordered.

Hailey frowned. She didn't want to do it. She knew deep inside her brain that something was terribly wrong. If she obeyed, she would hurt someone, though her brain refused to reveal who would be hurt. She had to stop this now.

The bag dangled over the edge, luffing in the night breeze like a sail in a faltering wind.

Let it go! The words ripped, sharp and commanding, so there could be no doubt of who was in control.

Hailey released the bag!

Minno slid on her belly to the ledge, clamping onto a strap just before it plummeted out of reach. With her other hand, she clutched the rock ledge to keep from toppling over with the bag.

Hailey shook herself awake.

"What are you doing down there?" she muttered. She drew the hair back from her face to see her toes dangling on the tip of the ledge. Forty feet below, a small fire flicked against the silver-tinted landscape. She gasped in terror, leaping backward and into Antinarra.

"What is this?" Antinarra demanded. She had only witnessed the last few moments, which terrified her in its implications.

Minno returned to her feet, slinging the bag back over her shoulder.

"Why did you do that?" Minno interrogated, shaking Hailey.

"Do what? I didn't do anything!"

"You almost lost the bag," Minno charged.

"No, I didn't." Hailey gazed around. "How'd I get here?"

"Yes, you did."

"Yo-kay. If you say so."

Antinarra opened Hailey's shirt collar to expose the silver neck band.

"The Chogga. How did Craveaux get it on her?" she asked, despair crowding her voice.

"Yeah, that. She tried it on. We can't get it off," Minno offered.

"This is very bad. Craveaux commands her. You must be careful," Antinarra replied.

"How do we get it off?"

"*We* don't," was all Antinarra said before corralling the girls back into the cavern.

26

Dawn crept over the horizon to the Oogly brothers stirring around a dying fire. Lying on her back, Moogly gazed up the sheer cliff at the hollow near the top. They had to reach that entrance. If they could, they could corner that little girl and seize the bag. Moogly fantasized about the power she could wield if she held that bag. She'd deal with Craveaux on her terms. Life for the Ooglys would become so much better *if* she controlled that bag.

Doogly turned to stare at her.

"There is only one way those little girls can leave that cave. They must come down to us. I say wait them out," he said, scratching under his arms.

"And if you're wrong, brother?"

Moogly's words forced Doogly to reassess. Could there be another exit from that cave? What were those little girls seeking anyway?

Foogly yawned loudly while scratching himself as he uncurled on the ground. Then he also gazed up the cliff.

"I'm hungry," he said, rummaging through his pockets for anything edible.

"Me, too," came from a Patsche, which was now less than ten paces from the Ooglys' camp.

"Who said that?" Foogly asked.

"Come on, let's find a way up that cliff," Moogly commanded, kicking dirt onto the last flickers of remaining fire.

Sachea and Minno walked through a tunnel leading to the morning's light. She had learned so much in the last few hours that everything inside her head felt jumbled and out of sorts. For the last nine years, as long as she could remember, she believed she was just another normal girl being raised by her grandfather. She had accepted that her parents were dead, and that her only family was her Grandpa Esri.

"Craveaux will try to trick you if he can, using half-truths to make you think he is not evil. Be wary. He will prey upon your youth and innocence," Sachea warned.

"I won't let him inside my head," Minno said.

"I hope not," Sachea replied surprised.

"Couldn't you have stayed human?"

Minno's question stopped Sachea in her tracks. Her eyes went misty.

"It broke our hearts to let you go. We loved you dearly. But we knew we would see you again. It had been foreseen by Desrilian. You would return to us, and we would be together."

"I just wanted to know what it felt like ..." Minno started. She struggled to find words to finish her thought.

"We are dragons, my child. It is what we are. It is who you are inside," Sachea said.

Antinarra joined them, having entered their tunnel from a descending side tunnel.

"It is time. You must go now," Antinarra said.

"What about the Ooglys? They're probably still waiting for us."

"They are no concern. They will not bother you," Antinarra said, leading Minno away.

Diverting to a descending tunnel into the darkness, in a moment, Sachea was gone. She chose not to say good-bye, fearing it might be their last words together. Minno felt an overwhelming need to run to her, to hug her. But she didn't. Sachea was her mother, that Minno understood for sure. And her mother needed to know she could count on Minno to help them.

"Your parents gave up everything important to them to save Ambrosia," Antinarra said.

"You mean they gave up their magic to save Ambrosia," Minno corrected.

"No, my dear, I mean they gave up *you* to save Ambrosia. Not a day has passed when your mother did not wonder what you had become," Antinarra pressed.

"I guess I didn't realize that."

"My dear, you are the Soma. All our fates rest in your hands," Antinarra said, drawing Minno out of her thoughts.

"What if I can't do it?"

Minno's question stung Antinarra so deeply she couldn't respond.

Reaching the cave entrance, they saw Gutty on his belly sliding back from the ledge, while Nole and Hailey knelt beside him.

"They're still there," Nole said. Defeat hammered at him even before they started their journey to the fortress.

"Yip. Won't be sneaking by 'em," Gutty added.

"Gutty, you couldn't sneak by a blind man. Don't suppose they'll give up?" Minno said.

"They're no longer a problem," Antinarra said. She pointed skyward. "Your transportation's here."

The four stared into the sky in amazement.

Four ten-foot, hard-shelled, Fanciewols circled in from high altitude. They resembled ladybugs mainly, except that they had long arching necks similar to a giraffe's, which allowed them to accommodate riders. However, their dispositions were anything but ladylike.

Nole's face paled. Gutty looked on confused. Minno tried to hide the terror rising into her face. Hailey was the only one excited at the sight. She broke into a beaming smile at the thought of riding one of those amazing creatures.

"Oh, no," was all Minno muttered.

"What?" Hailey asked.

"I don't think I can do this," Minno whispered so Antinarra wouldn't hear.

"You're afraid of ladybug thingies?" Hailey asked with surprise.

"No ... flying," Minno replied. She swallowed hard and wiped away sweat beading her brow. Her stomach cramped at the thought of being on one of those creatures and knowing the ground would be far below. But, as Antinarra had promised, it would eliminate the Ooglys as a problem.

The Fancies, as the creatures of Ambrosia called them, buzzed about, hovering above the cavern opening.

"Sure, giant ladybugs. I would have gone with giant butterflies, but I get it, short notice and all," Hailey said. She couldn't wait to get started.

"The Fancies will transport you to the Barrens," Antinarra said.

She receded back to the cave entrance to allow the Fancies space to hover at the ledge, and thus, allow the riders to mount. This flight would not be without its dangers, but it was the safest and most expeditious way to move the girls to their destination. There was less chance Craveaux could detect their approach to the fortress. They could remain out of soldiers' sight by traveling through the air rather than over land.

Hailey's Fancie had settled into boarding position and as a result had overheard Antinarra.

"The what!? I'm sorry, you talkin' to me? You talkin' to ME?" he said, sounding like the rude taxi driver everyone disliked.

"Sorry. The Fanciewols," Antinarra corrected.

It was unwise to upset a Fancie—especially when putting one's well-being on their wings after drafting them to perform a very dangerous mission. The Fancies hated Palladins as much, if not more, than the other creatures of Ambrosia. For many years Palladins hunted Fancies for their wings and necks. Many a soldier's hut proudly displayed colorful Fanciewol wings.

"Why do so few soldiers guard the Barrens?" Minno finally thought to ask.

Actually, she sought a reason to abandon their mission. She wanted to say they shouldn't go, that it was too dangerous to attempt it. Most of all, she wanted to keep from boarding a Fancie.

"Because nothing survives for long in the Barrens," Gutty said without trepidation. Then he leaned close to Minno.

"Great," Hailey muttered.

"Don't worry, I have the egg horn, remember?" he whispered. His eyes went to Hailey to make certain she had not overheard his words. Upon seeing the fear in Minno's eyes, he handed her his egg horn.

"This will keep you safe, I promise."

Minno handed it back.

"Then you must keep it."

She refused to accept it back.

But something more serious worried Gutty. Something even an egg horn could not help. The troll tugged Minno away from the others.

"This is too dangerous for Nole. If he falls asleep while on one of them ..."

Minno contemplated Gutty's concern.

"How else can he get there? We have to take that chance," Minno came back with. "How long do we have?"

"No one knows. He falls asleep when he falls asleep."

"I don't suppose those things have seat belts? What if we strap him to their back?"

"You go now. I will catch up. I must take care of things here," Gutty said.

Hailey mounted the first buzzing Fancie at the cavern opening.

"Hit the sky, Fancie bug!" Hailey cheered, waving a hand in cowgirl fashion. Inside, she was terrified. But she couldn't show fear in front of Minno. This was too important to her friend.

"Excuse me? You call me Fancie again, I'm gonna kick you tru 'dat rock over 'dere," Hailey's Fancie fired back.

They lifted off to circle overhead.

Minno still couldn't bring herself to mount hers. Her hands trembled at the thought.

"C'mon, move it, honey. We're burning daylight here," Minno's Fancie said. The words had little impact on Minno. Her knees had gone weak.

"You must do this, Minno," Antinarra said, "your parents are depending on you."

Minno swallowed. She climbed onto her ride and white-knuckled its long neck. Her eyes remained tightly closed as the Fancie buzzed out into a cloudless azure sky.

"Minno, you can do this. Just open your eyes but don't look down. Where's Gutty?" Hailey called as her Fancie banked into a tight circle, waiting for the others to join the formation.

The next Fancie swooped in. Nole readied himself.

"You must. He is helping us," Antinarra pleaded when the Fanciewol turned skittish.

Gutty removed the rope securing his trousers to use it around Nole and the Fancie's neck.

"What's that for?" the Fancie asked.

"Keep him safe," Gutty replied, pulling up drooping trousers.

"Fine. You so much as breathe wrong, I'll dump you into the trees, you got that, scum face?" the Fancie said.

Nole clung to the creature's neck.

"Your touch makes my spots crawl," the Fancie muttered before lifting off.

At the base of the cliff, the Ooglys packed their bags to make an ascent on the rock face. Foogly gazed up, hoping to find a way to scale it.

"See anything?" Moogly asked.

Foogly dashed from the wall at full pelt.

Splat!

He was too slow. Clods of mushy dragon poop rained down.

Moogly dove for cover, almost making it to safety beneath a tree.
Splat!

Another mushy scat boulder plopped onto Moogly's shoulder.

"Stinking troll! We'll get you," Doogly yelled, shaking a fist.

Gutty smiled down from the ledge. His dismissive wave infuriated the brothers even more.

"Lunch!" a Patsche yelled.

"Brilliant! I'm starving," another chimed.

"Ah, dragon poop again? More leftovers," another whined.

As the three Fancie's circled over the cliff, Gutty, aboard a super huge Fancie, came chugging over the edge with a faceful of smile.

"Way to go, Gutty. So long, Ooglys!" Hailey taunted.

The fancies circled one more time to form into their defensive flight formation before leaving the cliff, and the Ooglys, behind. Gutty's Fancie flapped as hard and as fast as she could, but still she couldn't keep pace with her comrades. Before long Gutty had fallen behind the others.

"Between you and the poop, I don't know which smells worse! Be careful with the shell back there, I just had it waxed," she said.

The Fancie huffed and puffed and finally reached the girls and Nole.

Deep inside the cavern, Sachea and Antinarra gazed at the glowing fish swimming in circles in the water.

"She's too inexperienced, too young," Antinarra said.

"Then we must find a way to help her."

"We are so few. What could we possibly do? Besides, we will be busy evading Craveaux's soldiers," Antinarra said.

For many moments neither spoke, each pondering in their own minds what they might do to turn the tide in their favor.

"Perhaps if we could distract Craveaux ..." Antinarra started.

"Yes! When his soldiers arrive, we will be long gone," Sachea said.

Antinarra's face displayed her surprise. Sachea had never dared leave this safe haven before. It was too dangerous to be caught in the open without her powers. That was exactly how Minno's father had fallen to Craveaux's dragon hunters.

"You said the only way to remain safe was to hide from Craveaux," Antinarra said.

"I believe that no longer. It is time to leave the darkness and rally behind the Soma."

"Where shall we go?"

"The one place Craveaux least expects us," Sachea said.

Sachea began moving, but not toward the depths of the cavern, rather toward the light at the cave's opening.

"Now is the time for all Ambrosians to embrace the Soma. Come, we have much to do."

Sachea arrived at the cavern opening with Antinarra at her side. Off in the distance, the Oogly brothers were cleaning up at a pond.

The Oogly brothers returned to their feet at the water's edge, cleansed of the dragon dung.

"We'll never track them now," Moogly complained. She panned the sky—the Fancies were long gone. Their bounty had slipped away, it would seem; but worse, so had Minno's magic bag.

"It's gone forever," Moogly moaned.

"We still have the egg horn," Doogly said.

Moogly smacked Doogly hard, which sent Foogly into a laughing fit. An egg horn was frivolous compared to the bag's power. As they left the pond, a black, silver-banded hummingbird swooped in to hover at Doogly's ear.

"Return to the fortress with all haste," Craveaux's voice commanded.

"How does he knows this stuff before we tells him?" Foogly muttered.

27

The four Fancies chugged along above the crown canopy of the Forest of Perpetual Stink. Hailey maintained her lead over the others, with Nole behind her and Minno a short distance behind him.

When Hailey looked back, she noticed Minno's eyes were still tightly closed while she death-gripped her Fanciewol's neck.

"Can we go faster?" Hailey prompted her Fancie. The surrounding air was still, quiet. No birds, and more importantly, no dragons shared the skies with them.

"What? You tink it's easy lugging a troll on your back. What is he, a ten-footer? We go only as fast as our slowest Fanciewol," Hailey's Fancie instructed.

Clustering kept them safe. Strength in numbers mattered most. At any moment, one or more might need to aid one of the others.

Hearing the words prompted Hailey to glance over her shoulder.

Gutty was gone!

"Gutty!" she called out with all the force she could muster. Panic spread through her. Her heart pounded. She should've taken the rear guard, allowing her to keep an eye on her troll friend.

"Ay, great, dis ain't good," Hailey's Fancie muttered, banking into a steep descent. "Hold on tight."

Moments later Hailey and her Fancie breached the forest canopy. Nole and Minno circled to follow. They had to stay together.

Stinging branches forced Minno's eyes open.

"What's happening? Where we going?" Minno stammered, clutching her Fancie more tightly.

"If you'd let me breathe, I'll tell you."

Minno relaxed her grip, albeit slightly, but enough to allow the Fancie to suck in deep breaths to speak.

"I see 'em. We got trouble," her Fancie called out.

"Big trouble, look!" Hailey called, pointing.

Nole swiveled, glimpsing Gutty in the trees.

Huge trouble!

General Furion's soldiers galloped full pelt after Gutty. And they were gaining, because Gutty's Fancie sputtered ten feet off the deck. Gutty's girth was just too much to carry for so long a journey. They had underestimated what it would take to transport the huge troll safely to the Barrens.

"We need to help them," Nole ordered his Fancie.

"No! She needs to jettison. The troll goes, so we can complete the mission," his Fancie argued back.

"I'm not leaving him. Get me in close to him."

"I'm not taking an arrow for a stinking Palladin. I'm out of here," Nole's Fancie said.

"Wait! Come in behind them. I'll help Gutty," Nole commanded, working to unfasten the rope binding him to the creature.

"How you gonna do that? You're tied to my neck."

"Not any more." He dangled the rope for his Fancie to see.

"Get me down there, then get yourself someplace safe."

His words surprised his Fancie. They revealed a concern for a creature other than himself, most unusual for a Palladin.

His Fancie pressed into a wobbly descent, falling into a line at the rear of the pursuing soldiers. It was the best the Fancie could do under the circumstances, though it was no help to the troll.

Up ahead, Gutty slapped his Fancie's behind, pressing for more speed.

"Hey! How'd you like it if I came up there and whacked your butt? Would it make you go faster?" Gutty's Fancie scowled in response.

"Sorry. Please go faster," Gutty apologized.

"That's better. Now hold on, fat boy, cuz we're kicking into vapor drive." Her wings accelerated into a frenzied overdrive. But the thundering hooves closing in drowned out the buzz of her desperate flapping.

She wove in and out of the trees, making it difficult for the archers to lock their shots on them, and forcing the soldiers to slow to constantly weave in and out. The maneuver was dangerous for a loaded-down Fancie, but it was their only chance for survival. One wrong bank, or an ill-timed weight shift, and *splat,* they're into a tree.

Slowly they were increasing their lead on the soldiers, but Gutty's Fancie began to falter—she couldn't maintain the breakneck pace for much longer. A few more moments would put the soldiers in range to take them down with a barrage of arrows.

Hailey's Fancie reacted, swooping in behind Gutty, matching their path exactly when the first bevy of arrows rained over their heads. Hailey screamed.

"Dis is gonna get ugly, sweetheart," Hailey's Fancie called back.

"Going to?" Hailey responded, tightening her hand on her Fancie's neck.

But Hailey suddenly smiled. A brilliant plan popped into her head. At her left flank, a ravine inspired an opportunity to save her friend.

"When I yell, you bank left, hard. Got it?"

"What? Why?"

"Just do it. We'll draw their fire. I need you to trust me."

"You crazy? Trust a Palladin? Gives me the heebie-jeebies."

Back at the rear of the charging soldiers, Nole's Fancie fell in beside the last straggling horseman. The soldier looked over in time to receive Nole's fist to his face, which came just before Nole abandoned his Fancie to seize the mount and topple the soldier. After fumbling to stay atop the galloping horse, Nole collected the reins and kicked the beast for maximum speed. He had to find some way to help Gutty.

But instead of pursuing the pack, the stallion slowed to a trot. Nole slumped forward in the saddle. His head drooped to rest on the animal's black mane. Untethered, the horse wandered off into the forest.

Nole's Fancie climbed out, retreating back the way they had come.

At the lead of the pack, Hailey knew she had to time her command to the precise second. If she broke too soon, the soldiers would realize her intent and avoid the ravine. If she broke late, they would have passed the ravine.

"Now!" she screamed to project her voice above thundering hooves.

Hailey's Fancie banked hard left, dipping in the turn, but she was able to maintain her altitude off the forest floor.

It worked!

The soldiers veered left, launching arrows wildly at her. Before they could realize it, the ground sloped sharply into the ravine and the horses followed, toppling into dense vegetation.

"Pull up with everything you've got!" Hailey commanded.

As her Fancie climbed into the treetops, she could see Gutty on his Fancie making a slow ascent ahead. Hailey spun, looking for Minno. At first, she was missing-in-action. Then she saw her clinging to her Fancie as the giant ladybug creature climbed, threading through drooping boughs.

On their ascent, a sea of thousands of bubbles floated through the branches. So many, that as they all popped, their words became jumbled together. Minno tried to unscramble the words into a coherent message. She could only hope the warnings in the bubbles were not meant for them, because they had no time to slow sufficiently to receive the words.

"Climb, Gutty, climb! Get us above the trees," Hailey chimed.

"Aye, aye, commander. Good job," Hailey's Fancie said.

Before breaching the crown canopy to reach the clear blue sky, Hailey took one more sweep in their wake. Nole was gone. She twisted back and forth, hoping to catch a glimpse of him. But there was nothing.

Once above the trees, Gutty's Fancie chugged along and eventually rejoined Minno, whose Fancie had slowed. Then Hailey broke through the foliage. Minno opened her eyes, clutching her Fancie's neck for dear life.

"Where's Nole?" Minno yelled across the void.

"He abandoned his Fancie for a horse. He's okay," Gutty reported.

"We're almost there, Minno. Just hang on," Hailey offered.

28

After three more hours in subdued flight, the Fancies left the treetops of the Forest of Perpetual Night and flew over the Barrens.

Below, a wasteland of smoldering rocks and viscous sand churned and groaned. The craggy ground and jutting rocks shifted continuously beneath them.

At irregular intervals, hot gas vents fired off like cannons, forcing the Fancies into dramatic ascents to avoid being burned alive. But Gutty's ride began to sputter—she couldn't hold altitude after many hours of hauling a huge load on her back.

Then, just when they thought they might make it, arrows whizzed by from the ridge of trees that marked the forest's edge. The projectiles strayed wide of their targets as the archers hidden somewhere below began to find their range.

"Oh, Gaaawd, archers. We got trouble," Minno's Fancie called out.

They hadn't expected to run up against them in the Barrens. Craveaux had become smarter. He had fortified his defenses against a weak-side attack.

Minno looked back to Gutty's floundering Fancie. As it dipped closer toward the ground, a blast of hot gas erupted. The Fancie's wing caught fire, flew off, sending Gutty's Fancie spiraling out of control.

Time slowed as they watched Gutty's ride plummeting toward the ground.

"Gutty! Nooooooo!" Hailey screamed.

She jerked her Fancie, steering it for Gutty. But it was too late.

In the next second, Gutty separated from the crashing Fancie, hurling toward the barren landscape.

"C'mon. We gotta hel ... GUTTY!" Hailey cried out in agony at watching the huge gentle troll falling into the Barrens.

As she watched helpless, the ground opened into a gaping mouth filled with rock teeth. It swallowed Gutty whole. But Gutty did not go down without a fight. He clawed the ground around him, desperate to pull himself out of the mouth. As he struggled, the collapsing orifice shut around him.

Gutty was gone.

"Noooo," Hailey cried. She steered her Fancie back to join Minno, who had gained on her.

More arrows arced in.

Most missed.

One found a soft spot under the wing of Hailey's Fancie.

"I'm hit. I can't hold altitude. You need to do something," Hailey's Fancie called. The Fancie struggled to maintain flight. But the harder it tried to flap its wings, the more agony it suffered.

"Minno, help!" Hailey cried out.

At first nothing happened. Minno, flying ahead, didn't turn her head. Maybe she couldn't hear Hailey's cries for help?

"Honey, you better do something, or you're gonna lose your friend," Minno's Fancie scolded. She took it upon herself to come about.

"Now!" Minno's Fancie screamed in anger.

By this time Hailey's Fancie fluttered dangerously close to the wasteland. A hot gas vent fired. Hailey's Fancie swerved right to avoid the lethal heat burst.

Minno opened her eyes. She saw Hailey going down so she grabbed tighter hold of her Fancie.

"I'm coming, Hailey. Hang on."

"Now you've got it, honey. Let's go rescue your friend," Minno's Fancie chimed. She banked into a steep dive to come beside Hailey's struggling Fancie.

"Grab my hand," Minno yelled when she came close enough to reach out for Hailey.

Hailey stretched as far as she could while still keeping one hand firmly on her Fancie. Her friend was still too far away.

"Get me closer," Minno commanded, which her Fancie obliged as best she could in the rough air over the Barrens.

"What do ya tink I'm tryin' to do?" Minno's Fancie complained. She worked her wings hard to slide in closer.

Hailey's fingers brushed Minno's.

Then they locked together.

Minno yanked with every ounce of strength she had.

Hailey left her plummeting Fancie, hopping in behind Minno on her Fancie.

"Hold on, ladies, I'm coming in low over that ridge," Minno's Fancie ordered as she leveled her wings like a glider attempting a smooth line toward the upcoming ridge.

A gas vent fired! It blasted them dead center from underneath, throwing the Fancie more than twenty feet skyward.

"I'm going down," Minno's Fancie whimpered with a fading breath.

The Fancie wobbled over the rock ridge. One of her wings ripped loose from her body.

Minno grabbed her bag, extending it over her head while praying her idea would work. They were out of options.

"Hold onto me," Minno yelled. She really didn't need to tell Hailey anything. Hailey clung to her and wasn't about to let go now.

Separating from the Fancie, Minno's bag popped into a parachute. They drifted over the rocks as their ride crashed a distance away. Then they swooped in for a gentle landing on the ridge.

A devastated Hailey sat on the rocky ground with tears streaming down her cheeks. "He's gone," she moaned.

Minno tried to comfort her, realizing they were still in the middle of the Barrens, and this was neither the time nor the place for mourning the loss of their friend. Like it or not, they *had* to get moving. Though at the present, Minno had no idea which was the right way to proceed.

"I wish I would have told him how much I liked him. You think he knew we cared about him?" Hailey said, wiping the tears away and bringing herself to her feet.

"He knew. He's the one who gave you your voice using those magic flowers," Minno revealed.

Hailey teared up again, sobbed anew.

"And I never thanked him."

Minno took her friend by her shoulders.

"I know this is hard. But we have to go. We don't have much time."

The words brought Hailey back to the danger around them. As they forged ahead, the rocks behind them formed into faces to follow their every move.

Feeling the eyes upon her, Hailey spun—saw only rocks.

"What's wrong?" Minno asked.

"This place is creeping me out. How much further?" Hailey retorted.

They crested the rock ridge to stare at the Barrens stretching before them. At the woody fringe on the opposite side of the expanse, they could see quartz spires jutting above the crown canopy.

"How could I possibly know that?" Minno snapped.

"You don't have to be snippy," Hailey shot back with equal ferocity.

"I liked him, too. But we need to f-o ... c-u-s-s-s-s-s!"

The ground beneath their feet swallowed them whole.

29

The girls tumbled head over heels down a twenty-foot rock slide, landing in a long and vaulted stone cavern. Shafts of sunlight seeped into the tunnel through the myriad of narrow cracks overhead.

"You okay?" Minno asked after coughing the dust out of her lungs and wiping her eyes so she could see.

Hailey coughed out her dust, afterward checking her ankles, knees and finally elbows.

"Nothin' broken. Any idea where we're at?" Hailey asked, glad to see that enough light seeped in to illuminate the path ahead.

"Yeah, I know exactly where we're at," Minno said. She brushed off her clothes and trekked into the tunnel.

"Seriously?"

Minno turned back and just looked at her.

"Well, how should I know?" Hailey added.

The girls advanced deeper into the descending tunnel.

"You could've just said no," Hailey sniped.

"Let's hope this leads to the fortress."

As the girls marched deeper into the tunnel, the Stalactites in their wake began extending downward to mesh with the Stalagmites rising off the floor.

"There's an opening down there," Hailey offered.

"I see it. Maybe it leads into the fortress," Minno added.

When Minno glanced back at Hailey, she noticed the path they had traveled had been sealed off by the Stalactites and Stalagmites.

"I hope it does, because there's no turning back now."

Hailey gasped when she looked back.

"We're trapped in here."

"Yeah, that's pretty much the situation," Minno offered. When she turned back to proceed down the tunnel, she slammed right into a huge boulder now blocking her path.

"This wasn't here a second ago," Hailey said, suddenly afraid to take another step.

When Minno sidestepped to circumvent the boulder, another rolled in to impede her progress.

"O-kay. Looks like we're dealing with some pretty smart rocks," Minno said intentionally loud, wanting the rocks to hear. That is, if they could hear. Since they could move, maybe they could hear every word.

Minno motioned Hailey to advance. Her shift brought a rock tumbling from the sidewall across her path. Using her hand, Hailey signaled to Minno that she was going over the rock.

"Yeah, these smart rocks are making it impossible for us to move down this tunnel. I guess we're stuck here," Minno said.

When she nodded, Hailey braced against the sidewall before setting a foot on the fallen rock. The surface beneath her hand morphed into a gaping mouth poised to chomp down on her fingers.

So intense was Hailey's concentration that she failed to see the rock about to crush her fingers.

"Hailey, jump now!" Minno screamed.

Hailey's hand recoiled off the wall just before the mouth closed. Her momentum carried her safely over the fallen rock into the center of the tunnel.

Minno dodged left to leap over the fallen rock in Hailey's wake. Ahead, rocks shifted en mass, separating from the walls to form a maze.

"We need to run, now!" Minno shouted. She assumed the lead from Hailey. They dashed down the tunnel, weaving in and out and around shifting boulders that quickly closed in behind them.

At last, they reached an opening. But a large circular granite slab angled down to seal off the passage. Minno hit her belly to slide through. Hailey followed a moment later, snapping her knees to her chest a split second before the giant slab sealed them off from the tunnel.

For seconds neither moved. They made it through the maze. But neither knew where they were. The girls shifted to a sitting position against the rock wall, gasping. Then they slapped each other a high-five.

"We just outwitted a bunch of rocks. Should we really be excited?" Minno said.

"We outwitted smart rocks, so yeah, we should."

After a few minutes their racing hearts returned to normal. The beaded sweat on their foreheads sent chills through their bodies. Hailey pulled her knees up to wrap her arms around her shins. She rested her chin on her knees.

"You're not gonna turn into a dragon, are you?," she asked, gazing straight ahead rather than to meet her friend's eyes.

"What?"

"Well, your parents are dragons. Maybe you're going to turn into one."

"Why would you think that?"

"Duh?"

"They were humans when they had me."

"But they're not now."

"Where is this going, Hailey?"

"I just don't want to lose my only friend. Oh, God, how pathetic did that sound."

"I'm not going to turn into a dragon. But they are my parents."

"Hey, I'm not judging. I mean it's not like you can take them back with you after this is over. Do you really think they're going meet with your teacher on Parents Night at Blue Lake Middle School?"

Minno offered no response.

"And what do you think your boyfriend is going to say when he meets your parents? Cool, your parents are dragons."

"I don't have a boyfriend."

"Well, not yet. We're going to be famous when we do return to Blue Lake. Every boy in school is going to want to talk to us."

"Do you honestly think anyone is going to believe us when we tell them about where we've been?"

"No, but we've got pictures. Remember your cell phone?"

"Yeah, that got trashed in the water. We don't have any pictures for proof," Minno countered.

"Great. The adventure of a lifetime and not one shred of proof to show what we did."

Minno pulled herself up, brushed herself off and began her trek down the tunnel toward the light. Hailey pulled herself up a moment later to catch up to Minno.

"You realize nobody's going to mess with you when they find out your parents are dragons. How cool is that?"

Minno just looked at her.

"Never mind what I said," Hailey offered in apology.

The girls had walked a few hundred paces when they saw the light brightening at the end of the tunnel.

"Cool, the light at the end of the tunnel," Hailey said, laughing.

The light at the end of the tunnel actually formed into, what else, a gaping mouth with rows of rock teeth jutting out from the rock wall.

"That doesn't look so good," Hailey said.

Minno stopped, tightening on Hailey's arm.

"I'm thinking all these rocks, they're some kind of security system for the fortress."

"Yeah, so?"

"So, through that opening could be where we want to go. Besides it's a hole in the wall, right?"

"Yeah, but it's a hole in the wall with teeth. Do we go through it?"

"I'm not sure," Minno said.

Hailey advanced a few more steps. A rock at the sidewall turned into a hand reaching out to swat at her. She screamed, leaping beyond its reach. Both girls gravitated to the center of the tunnel, keeping as far away from the walls as possible.

"I guess we're going through that opening," Hailey said.

"It's the only way out," a gruff voice somewhere overhead said. It sounded like it came from everywhere around them.

"Who said that?" Minno asked.

The sidewalls transformed into a hundred smiling faces.

"*GAAAAHHHHHHH!*" the rock wall uttered.

Hailey screamed.

"Run!" Minno yelled.

But they didn't run far. Approaching the lighted opening, they saw skeletal remains littering the inside of the mouth: a few large troll skulls and leg bones, along with man-size rabbit skeletons that were intermingled amongst a small dragon's rib cage and tail bones.

"Why do you come here?" the rock face asked.

The girls detected no movement among the rock faces. The voice had come from somewhere deep inside the tunnel.

"To enter Craveaux's fortress," Minno said calmly, as if nothing could shake her confidence.

"First you must solve the riddle," the rock face responded.

"Then tell me the riddle, so we may pass unharmed," Minno replied.

"So, now we're going to *trust* a rock," Hailey said out the side of her mouth.

"Zip it," Minno scolded.

"Only one in Ambrosia can set you free, and destroy the evil that lurks on high."

"I don't suppose that was in the book your Grandpa Es ..." Hailey started. She couldn't complete it, because Minno clamped a hand over her mouth.

"We can't afford any mistakes. We must choose our words carefully, okay?"

Only after Hailey nodded approval did Minno release her hand.

"Could he be looking for the Soma?" Hailey whispered.

"Which part of what I just said did you *not* understand? If we answer incorrectly and can't change our answer, we could end up like those creatures. Besides, that could be the obvious answer. No one here knows who the Soma is."

But it's..."

Hailey's mouth got clamped once more. After a second, Minno released it.

"Focus. It said the evil that lurks on high," Minno offered.

"It's the dragons. It's Desri ..." Hailey began.

"Craveaux! The answer is Craveaux," Minno blurted, drowning out Hailey's words.

"You may enter," the rock face said.

Both girls heaved a great sigh. Hailey ventured forward. Minno took her first step to follow her.

"If you are correct, you will not die," the rock face added.

"Great. Are you sure?" Hailey asked, pausing in her tracks.

Minno answered by entering the gaping mouth. Together they gingerly stepped over the bones of the previous invaders.

The rock mouth began to close! Hailey screamed.

The girls dashed through the mouth, springing over the bones and into another tunnel feeding into another distant light.

The rock face laughed boisterously.

Once safely inside, the girls leaned against the tunnel wall, breathing heavily. Then they laughed and slapped their hands together.

"How did you know?" Hailey asked.

"Simple. Who created the riddle? Craveaux. His ego is all over this place. He thinks of himself as the savior of the creatures, rather than the one destroying them."

"Good point."

"C'mon," Minno said.

She resumed walking with a determined bounce in her step.

"What if they're waiting for us?" Hailey called. She hurried to catch up.

"You're really a buzz kill, you know that? Besides, no one knows we're here," Minno reasoned.

30

Minno led Hailey through a narrow crevasse which opened into another chamber. They had yet to reach the source of the light, but they were definitely getting closer. Minno extracted a lighted torch from a wall stanchion, shoving it to arm's length for a better look at what lie ahead. What they saw froze their feet to the floor.

"Oh, yeah, no one knows we're here," Hailey mocked. She tried to swallow but couldn't. They had successfully come this far, only to now stand on the verge of being captured by Craveaux's men, check that, Craveaux himself.

The high minister stepped into the flickering light. The Oogly brothers crowded behind him. All wore sinister smiles.

"Foolish little girls. You came back. And you brought your bag," Craveaux said casually. "Surrender the dragon wing, and you both go free." The high minister's voice turned grim.

"You know I can't do that," Minno replied with the same coolness. She knew she could never allow Craveaux to intimidate her.

Hailey couldn't believe the girl standing beside her could remain so stoic in this situation. Hailey thought she was about to pee her pants. Or at the very least, upchuck anything in her stomach.

The high minister made no reply. Minno was expecting him to try another approach. Instead, he removed a hand-sized, hairy spider from beneath his robe. He paused for a few seconds, smiling before setting the creature on the rock floor between them.

"Then too bad for you."

"We're not afraid of spiders," Minno said.

"Speak for yourself," Hailey injected, though she realized it might be best if she remained quiet. The tension between them escalated with each breath. No one moved. Not even the spider. The Oogly brothers, however, began salivating.

Then in a blinding flash, Craveaux zapped the spider with blue lightning from his hand. The Ooglys retreated to disappear into the tunnel from which they came, with the high minister following a moment later.

Intuition warned Minno not to be alone with the spider.

"Okay. This is gonna be bad," Hailey said, trying to tamp down her rising panic.

Right before their eyes, the spider began churning and stretching. It morphed into a hairy, clawed monster, with bioluminescent green eyes. Baring two rows of drooling ivory fangs, it easily reached fifteen feet tall by the time the transformation completed. Then it hammered a vicious roar off the rock chamber walls.

Hailey looked to Minno in terror. She commanded her feet to run—nothing happened.

Minno knew in an instant that thing was the same kind of creature that had attacked her grandpa back in Blue Lake.

The girls ducked into the tunnel enclave from which they emerged, hoping the creature's sheer size would prevent it from following.

In a matter of seconds they had thirty paces between them and the Arachnorock.

"That thing took Grampa Esri," Minno said, not with fear in her voice, but with a newfound fierce determination.

"Oh, now you're not afraid. Maybe we should go back," Hailey stammered.

Minno gave her a look, and Hailey knew her friend would not be backing down from this fight.

"Okay, fine. Just tell me your magic bag has something that destroys that thing."

Back inside the chamber, the Arachnorock sniffed in rapid bursts for the girls' scents, then it roared again with such resounding force that the girls' teeth reverberated from the shock waves. Through the tunnel opening, they watched as the Arachnorock inhaled deeply to spray green fire down the tunnel.

Instinctively the girls huddled behind the bag, which expanded into a parabolic heat shield deflecting the flames. Without fuel to burn, the fire quickly evaporated, leaving only iridescent green eyes in the darkness.

Then the Arachnorock disappeared.

The girls looked at each other confused for a moment.

"He probably thinks we're french fries," Minno said.

"How do you know it's a he?" Hailey asked, which struck Minno as odd that she would even think to ask such a question at a time like this.

"Does it matter?" Minno replied.

"I'm just asking. Thought maybe you knew how to tell the sex of that thing. You seem to know everything else."

"No, I don't," Minno said.

"Well, you act like you do," Hailey insisted.

"I do not."

"Oh, I suppose you've never ever stopped to listen to yourself . . ."

"Okay, now you're starting to sound like a brat. We don't have time for this. Let's move. We have to get past that thing to reach the dungeon," Minno instructed.

"Right. We're heading to the dungeon. We really should start going to nicer places," Hailey said as she ran to catch up to her friend.

Minno led them into a vaulted open cavern with a twenty-foot ceiling crowded with Stalactites. Torchlight played off the walls and the shallow pools of standing water. Dripping sounds and plopping feet broke the still.

"This is crazy. That thing's coming back," Hailey said.

"Maybe not. Maybe it thinks we're fried and returned to its web."

"Its web? Can you even fathom how large its web must be to hold something that huge? And I thought Gutty was overweight," Hailey countered.

"Okay, maybe not its web. Maybe it went back to its lair. Is that better?" Minno corrected.

"Oh, yeah, way better. I'm not hardly even scared anymore."

The green eyes emerged from a side tunnel. The Arachnorock released a roar that shook boulders loose from the walls, blasting into the girls' ears. Both girls screamed.

"Run!" Minno yelled.

Hailey had already figured that out. She raced ahead of her friend to slip through a crack in a side wall.

The Arachnorock spun to find Hailey, lowering its gruesome head so the glowing octagon eyes could search for her at ground level.

"Hey, you, eight-legged freak! I'm over here," Minno called out, hoping to divert the creature from Hailey.

And, of course, it worked.

The Arachnorock came about to locate Minno. Minno dove behind a jagged boulder just an instant before a fire stream bounced off the rock and evaporated. She worked her bag off her shoulder before peering around the boulder's edge to get a bead on where the monster had gone.

Hailey bolted from the crack to escape down a low narrow tunnel, one certainly too narrow for the Arachnorock to even fit its ugly head through.

"Minno, this way. That thing can't fi..." Hailey blurted.

A grimy hand smothered her words. She yanked it away just long enough to spew a terrified scream and a few unintelligible words. The hand silenced her again, while another crumpled her collar, dragging her into the black void.

"Hailey! Hailey!" Minno screamed out. She hoped to capture a sound that might help her determine which direction Hailey had gone off.

Still behind the jagged boulder, Minno search frantically ... there had to be some way to get by the Arachnorock. In a desperate move, she fired a large rock at the beast—it did nothing.

Then she placed another rock, this one much larger than the first, into the center of her closed bag. Using the bag like a sling, she whirled it over her head then released one of the straps. The rock hurled like a missile, whacking the Arachnorock's head, sending the creature into dizzying gyrations. The beast roared in anger. Thick viscous drool slithered off its fangs.

"Take that, fire-breathing Jerkface!" Minno taunted from behind the boulder. Yet for all her effort, she had only achieved making the monster angrier and more determined to get her.

The beast shook off its dizziness, regained its bearings and closed in on Minno.

"Okay. New plan," she muttered. Her mind raced through her options. She was running out of time. Sooner rather than later that beast would attack, and she was going to need to get by that thing. Something more powerful than a large rock was called for to bring the beast down. Then her mother's words jumped to the front of her brain. The bag she carried wielded powers far greater than anything she could imagine.

Maybe this was a moment to test the limits of that power. Her mind raced. She searched for something that could help her fend of the Arachnorock's assault.

A burst of fire hit the boulder, curling around it, but vanishing before reaching Minno. She feared the next fire burst would reach her.

The Arachnorock shifted into the center of the open cavern. He settled beneath a large Stalactite, one whose girth matched the beast's head. Seeing that spawned an idea. She'd get one shot, and it better be good, but there was a chance it could work.

Minno peered out from behind the boulder just long enough to size up her plan. A burst of fire hitting the boulder forced her back.

"Please work. You have to make this work," she said, uncertain if the bag could understand what she was saying, if it even heard her.

Minno inched away from behind the boulder long enough to roll another waist-high rock onto her bag. The bag flattened out to accommodate the boulder's size. Then, as if that huge boulder were made of foam, Minno lifted it using the bag's straps. She began to swing it in a wide arc over her head.

She came around the boulder protecting her, and before the monster could react, she released a strap, allowing the huge projectile on her bag to sail toward the creature.

Her shot went high over the Arachnorock's head, which brought a menacing laugh from the beast. But the Arachnorock shouldn't have laughed.

Minno's intent was not to strike the Arachnorock. Rather, the boulder nailed the Stalactite protruding directly above the creature's head, cracking it from the ceiling.

The ensuing moment seemed endless. The Arachnorock stared at Minno, who smiled, throwing the bag over her shoulder.

With a grunt the Arachnorock inhaled.

"Uhhh-uhhh," Minno said, pointing up.

The Arachnorock looked up one second before the Stalactite slammed into its head, sending the beast crashing to the rock floor.

"That's for my grampa Esri. Hailey!"

Minno dashed around the now lifeless beast.

"And I thought trolls smelled bad."

Then she disappeared into the narrow tunnel where she believed Hailey had gone.

31

The Oogly brothers filed into an open chamber at the core of a maze of tunnels beneath the fortress with Hailey in their clutches. Doogly plopped her forcefully into an oversized wooden chair, then he leaned in menacingly over her. They were nose-to-nose. The stench wafting off Doogly's body grew unbearable. Hailey pasted on her toughest face. Doogly took to sniffing her.

"Please don't do that. Do you even know how annoying that is? How would you like if I sniffed you? Quite frankly, that very thought is making me ill."

"We know about the magic bag," Doogly said. His eyes came back up to lock onto hers. He wanted to savor the fear in her eyes.

Hailey disappointed him.

"Yo-kay. You'd be pretty dumb not to, considering." Her voice trailed off. She hoped her timidity might get them to ease up on her. She had no idea what to expect from these gophers for Craveaux.

Moogly moved in for a turn.

"You think we're toying with you? You think this is all some fun game?" Moogly delivered slow and easy. The hard edge in her voice unnerved Hailey.

"You mean it's not?" Hailey offered. However, her shaky words lacked force and conviction. The Oogly brothers were getting inside her head. And once they were there, Hailey didn't know if she could get them out.

Moogly stepped back, allowing Doogly to press in closer.

Hailey kicked Doogly's shin, pushing him into his brothers while she bolted for the chamber opening. She fled no more than five strides before writhing in pain while crumpling to her knees. She clutched at her neck. Tears stole her vision. The intense pain electrifying every fiber of her being made a scream impossible.

Craveaux entered with a hand outstretched.

"You will sit back down now," he ordered calmly, deliberately pausing between each word.

Hailey dutifully returned to her feet, pulling at the Chogga around her neck. Against all her resistance and her will to oppose him, she returned meekly to the chair to face Doogly.

Craveaux stared right at her with his eyeless sockets. How that was even possible, Hailey couldn't fathom. He crossed his arms and closed in next to her.

"You'll be dinner for the spiders," Craveaux said matter-of-factly. It didn't come out like a threat—more like a certainty, if she failed to do exactly what he asked of her.

Hailey's quivering lower lip and fake tear suggested she might crumble at his next word.

Craveaux's face softened.

Hailey broke into a laugh.

"How do you do that anyway?" she asked when she could think of nothing else to say. She knew she had zero control over this situation. Her only hope was Minno had escaped the monster in the tunnels and was on her way here right now. If she wasn't . . .

Craveaux turned a vicious eye, or rather a vicious eye socket, to Hailey.

"You have no idea what you have, do you?" the high minister asked, not expecting an answer.

Hailey responded with a confused expression on her face.

"One totally worthless cell phone, some pocket lint and twenty-seven cents. I know exactly what I have. Oh, you really didn't want an answer, did you?"

Shaking her to get her attention, Craveaux then grabbed a fistful of hair, forcing Hailey to look into his sockets.

"Why would you return to the fortress?" the high minister pondered aloud. Their presence had a more profound meaning, but as yet he couldn't uncover it.

"Isn't this where we catch the number thirteen bus ..." Hailey spit back.

"Silence!" Craveaux yelled. Then he paused. "Surrender the bag and you'll return safely to your lake that is blue."

"I think you mean Blue Lake. You're really having a hard time with that concept. And it's not actually a lake, you know. What about my friend?"

"Do you *really* care what happens to her?" Craveaux queried.

"Okay, I'll bite. Suppose I don't?"

The Oogly brothers growled.

"We seed her use that bag of hers," Foogly interrupted.

"You *saw* her use it. You don't seed something. Sheesh, and I'm the little girl. Right."

Moogly shoved Foogly aside to get into Hailey's face, issuing a guttural wolfish growl.

"You think it's funny?" Moogly asked, peering into her eyes.

"You mean like funny ha, ha, or funny, like you don't want to be looking at me like that?"

The question stymied Moogly.

"Why would you return?" Craveaux asked, standing only inches from Hailey. He doled out his words more as if he were querying himself rather than the little girl.

Hailey attempted to stare Craveaux down, but his grotesquely scarred face and extremely bad breath forced her to turn away.

"You people don't have toothpaste here, do you?"

Seeing her reaction, Craveaux shoved Moogly to come in close to Hailey's face.

"It is best you say what Craveaux wants to hear."

"My lips are sealed," Hailey offered plainly.

"Don't you wish to go home? Surely people are waiting for you?"

"We know what you're doing! Shoot," Hailey blurted out.

That strange, diabolic voice inside her head took over again. It made demands—she responded. She couldn't even explain why she said what she did. It just flew out of her mouth when she wasn't paying attention. Maybe she wanted Craveaux to know she wasn't the innocent little girl he thought her to be. Then maybe it was the high minister inside her head making her do it.

Hailey clamped her mouth shut.

"You do?" Craveaux toyed. A wicked smile spread across his face.

Now Foogly and Moogly also crowded Hailey's face.

"What is Craveaux doing?"

The high minister knew he was fracturing Hailey's resistance. Soon she would tell him anything, and everything, he wanted to know.

"Remove this thing from around my neck, and I'll tell you anything you want to know."

Craveaux pondered her offer. He knew all he had to do was look at her crossly and she'd wilt like a daisy on a hot day. The high minister took pleasure knowing he struck terror into her heart so effortlessly. For a brief moment he wondered if the other little girl, the one more important than this one, would wilt as easily under his control. He hoped he might be moments away from finding out. That is, if the Arachnorock hadn't already disposed of her.

"No," slipped out the corner of Hailey's mouth before Craveaux could respond. Trying to remain silent, Hailey's face contorted as she held her breath.

"She's one tough nut to crack," Moogly said.

After a few more moments, Hailey squinted, bobbing her head until finally, she could take it no more.

"You're killing the dragons to steal their magic," Hailey blurted, pausing to draw in a revitalizing breath. "My lips are sealed. Who am I kidding? I haven't talked for twelve years. My lips are totally unsealed."

"So that's what you think Craveaux is doing in his fortress?" The words caused the high minister to ponder momentarily before smiling.

"This one is birdie in the head," Doogly commented.

"Look who's talking, if birdie means what I think it means," Hailey retorted. "We're going to stop you," she offered to Craveaux.

"So, you've come to free the dragons?"

"I never said that. Did I say that? Wait. No, I never said that. I should just stop talking now."

"That's it, we might as well just give up. She'll never break," Moogly said.

Craveaux backed away. Perhaps these little girls could be more useful to him than he had originally imagined. If the creatures in

Ambrosia believed he was stealing the magic from the dragons, it might be valuable if he did nothing to change that belief.

"Send every soldier to guard the dragons, and lock this one in my chamber," the high minister commanded.

Then, to show his good faith, Craveaux reached around Hailey's neck, where with two fingers and a bluish spark, he removed the Chogga that bound her to his will.

"You see, Craveaux is not so evil."

The high minister shifted his attention to his three minions, all standing ready to serve.

"Bring Craveaux the bag and dispose of the girl."

"Yes, high minister, as you bid," Moogly said.

But the Oogly brothers all stood dumbfounded.

"Repeat it back to Craveaux," he commanded.

"Right. Send soldiers to guard the dragons, lock you in your chamber, bring the girl and dispose of the bag. We got it," Moogly doled out with confidence.

"No! Lock *her* in Craveaux's chamber. Send soldiers to guard the dragons. Bring Craveaux the bag and dispose of the girl."

Doogly stepped up.

"Got it," he said.

"Got it!" Foogly chimed in right after.

Moogly, however, hesitated, pondering her response.

"Bring you the soldiers ... ah ... something about your chamber, get the girl, ah ... but dispose of the, ah, bag..."

"Just do as Craveaux commands!"

"Yes, high minister," Doogly said, saluting with his left hand.

Craveaux stormed out. In the meantime Doogly struggled to get it all straight inside his head.

"You heard his high greatness. Nows move!" Foogly commanded.

The three collided in the middle of the chamber, all clamoring to dash out to find Minno and her powerful bag. So excited were they at the prospect of a possible reward, that none gave Hailey a thought.

Suppressing her smile, Hailey remained perfectly still, not even breathing, until after the Ooglys had disappeared. Then she giggled out loud, but she caught herself and silenced her noise with a hand to her mouth.

"God, they really are stupid," she whispered.

A moment later she darted into a tunnel leading away from the Oogly brothers. She hoped Minno had survived the monster and now she had to stop her friend from going to the dungeon.

32

Minno moved fluidly down one dark tunnel, leaving it for a crossing tunnel. She waited, easing back out of the torchlight when the rumble of marching feet rose. Her heart raced. The feet were closing in on her. In a few seconds they would be on top of her. But the soldiers passed oblivious to her, continuing down a tunnel leading away.

For now she was safe.

She proceeded into the tunnel in their wake. But a few steps later, the sounds of feet spun her around ready to fight. Her arms flailed in wild gyrations. She thought more soldiers had come up behind her.

"Easy, Kung Fu Panda. It's me," Hailey said, throwing her arms up to protect herself.

Minno hugged Hailey so tightly that neither could breathe. She believed she had lost her friend to Craveaux for good.

"Thank God you're okay. What happened?" Minno asked, hardly comprehending that Hailey was safe.

"The Ooglys and Craveaux grabbed me," Hailey said coolly.

"And you escaped? Excellent."

They high-fived each other.

"Not really, those Oogly brothers are really quite dumb."

"I wonder where those soldiers are going?" Minno asked.

"Oh, yeah, that. To the dungeon ... to guard the dragons."

"Why would they be doing that?" Minno's brow turned up.

"Uhhh, yeah, about that ... we need to move to get there before them."

"What did you do?"

"Craveaux made me talk. It was terrible, horrible torture, Indian burns, noogies, and ... I couldn't stand the pain."

"He tortured you?" Minno asked, aghast.

"No. No, not exactly. But he made me look at his eye sockets. That's torture."

"Come on then. We don't have much time." Minno slogged into the tunnel in the soldiers' wake.

"Oh, now you don't have time to talk. We just spent what, five minutes chatting, and now that I feel a need to talk, we gotta go. Great."

Hailey ran to catch up to Minno in the tunnel.

After navigating a series of tunnels that turned to the left and to the right, the girls saw bright lights ahead. They could also detect male grumbling voices.

Hailey and Minno stopped short of the dungeon area. They could see the soldiers milling around before the huge timber doors secured with chains and the giant lock. The men paid little attention to the tunnels. This was the same place Minno and Hailey first heard the screeching sounds when they escaped the fortress with Gutty's help.

For a moment, the memory brought Gutty's face to Minno's mind. She recalled the way he gazed up at them from the ground in the forest where they first exited the portal. He had saved them more times than they had saved him along the way. But now he was gone. And they had to do this for him. They had to make things right in Ambrosia.

"So, how's this gonna work?" Hailey asked, drawing Minno back to the present.

For a long, excruciating moment, Minno just stared blankly at her. The dungeon doors, the huge lock, a dozen soldiers with spears or swords hanging around the open expanse, was she crazy to think she could find a way to free the dragons? They could never succeed in such a wild task.

"You have no clue, do you?" Hailey persisted when no answers seemed forthcoming.

"Well, first of all, I wasn't expecting all those soldiers," Minno finally admitted, surrendering her thoughts to the armed men twenty paces away.

"Yeah, my bad," Hailey apologized.

"It's gonna be dangerous now."

Minno stalled for time to conjure up a plan. There had to be a way past the soldiers. But even after that, what about that lock?

"No, really? I figured that much out," Hailey said, "I'm not stupid, you know."

"I didn't say you were. I would never think you're stupid," Minno shot back.

"You know, you can say someone's stupid by saying something that makes them look stupid, without actually saying their stupid ..." Hailey badgered.

"Sshh! You ever think maybe they are?"

"Are what?"

"Stupid! All those men might be no smarter than the Oogly brothers."

"Yo-kay. I follow so far. So what do we do?"

"Right. One of us creates a diversion, allowing the other to get the doors open."

"Wow, that's so simple. Why didn't I think of that ... not!" Hailey mocked sardonically. She spent a few seconds sizing up the huge lock at the doors.

"So how does your great plan get a gigantic key, which is necessary to open the monster lock and those chains on the doors?" Hailey replied.

Minno bit at her lower lip while her mind raced through options that might help them succeed. She did see one advantage in their favor.

"It's an old lock. Can't be hard to pick," Minno said.

"It's huge!" Hailey started to assert, then she thought about what Minno had said. "You know how to pick a lock?" she added, genuinely surprised. "Had you pegged as Ms. goodie-goodie girl, who never does anything bad."

"No, I don't know how to pick a lock. But if you shove something in deep enough and turn, it should open, right?"

Hailey's face turned up in confusion.

"Yeah, this is a pretty lame plan. Oh, one other thing. If someone doesn't have eyes, can they still give you the stink eye?"

"The what?"

"I think Craveaux gave me the stink eye when he had me back there."

"Can we just focus on this problem. Besides, I've got my bag."

"Oh, yeah, about that. Craveaux knows about the bag."

"You *told* him about the bag!" Minno's voice rose an octave in anger.

"Not exactly. I mean, he guessed a lot of it himself."

"Can we stay on the diversion?"

Hailey bolted for the huge doors.

"Y-o-o-o-o k-k-k-k-a-y-y!"

She entered the dungeon area without thinking about what she would do once arriving there. She figured she'd think of something on the way, except after ten steps, she was there and still had not formulated a diversion she thought might work.

"What ... wait!" Minno called out.

It was way too late to stop her friend.

Hailey paused right there in the middle of the dungeon area. Two dozen eyes turned to her. At first, none of the soldiers knew what to make of her. The only children allowed in the dungeon area were either prisoners, or those in training as bait for dragon or troll hunters. And children-in-training were never allowed to roam free without a handler in tow.

"Which way is the pool? Is it next to the gift shop? This place gets so confusing," she said, staring deadpan at the armed men.

She then dashed toward a tunnel.

Not a single soldier took up the chase, forcing Hailey to stop and spin about to face them.

"Hel-lo, dumbos. I'm the one Craveaux is looking for. Any of you dimwits want the huge bounty he's placed on me? It's a biggie!"

The soldiers fell all over each other to pursue her.

After a few seconds of pounding feet, the dungeon became devoid of life. Minno emerged from the tunnel, forcing deep breathes to calm her racing heart. Wasting no steps, she crossed to the huge lock. It suddenly looked a lot larger than she thought.

"Piece a cake!" she heard Hailey call out from down one of the tunnels.

High-pitched dragon screeching rose the moment Minno reached the lock.

"Quiet! I'm the Soma, and I'm here to free you," she said to the doors. She could only wonder if they could hear her through the massive timber planks.

She next climbed onto the massive lock securing the chains so she could squirm her way through the keyhole. For the first few seconds inside, she just took everything in. Levers, gears, and an iron bar that held the lock mechanism closed. She had expected it would be a more simple device than what she was seeing. Her eyes followed the iron bar back to the keyhole via the gears and levers.

She quickly surmised that turning the gears until they pushed their adjacent levers up would release the iron bar and disengage the locking arm.

"Which one do I do first?" she muttered. She couldn't determine if the sequence she followed mattered. So she shoved the closest lever—it rotated a gear that nudged the iron bar slightly.

"Yes!" she chimed.

Her plan was totally working. All she had to do was continue pushing levers and gears until the locking mechanism released. She pushed another, which rotated a larger gear that slid the bar even more.

Annoying sweat trickled down her cheeks. The heat inside the lock made breathing difficult. But she was making progress, and after wiping her eyes, she pushed the first lever again. As it moved, sounds outside in the dungeon filtered in. She stopped, held her breath. At great risk, she peeked out the keyhole.

Hailey came dashing back into the dungeon area.

"What are you doing?" Minno snapped.

Hailey spun about, confused.

"Oh, dragon poop. I made a wrong turn."

Hearing pounding feet, Hailey wiggled in through the keyhole to join Minno. The confining space inside the lock mashed the two girls tightly together, forcing them to work their arms over each other.

"We both can't fit," Minno eeked out while squirming to one side, allowing her to move her left arm.

"I know that now," Hailey informed her, threading to the other side and stretching her arms overhead.

The rabble of grumbling men seized the girls. Flickers of movement crossed the keyhole. This was not good. Fortunate for them, no soldiers thought to inspect the keyhole.

"Help me push," Minno whispered.

Each girl shoved a lever as hard as she could. The locking bar slid further. The mechanism held an inch from releasing the locking arm. Their next push had to be slow and very deliberate, so as not to alert the soldiers. Their desperate action, however, forced a lever to slip off a gear, trapping Minno's forearm against an iron plate.

"What now?" Hailey pressed in a whisper. She could see the pain in Minno's eyes.

Minno grimaced. Searing agony fired through her muscles into her shoulder. She shifted away from the lever hoping to free her arm. That didn't work. Her forearm remained trapped. Minno's eyes tracked along the lever, up to the gear then over to the release arm.

"Climb onto my knee ... put all your weight against that lever there," she said, indicating a lever inches beyond their reach.

Hailey complied without retort, seeing the growing agony in Minno's eyes. There as no blood at the moment, but Hailey knew before long the iron bar would cut into her friend's skin. She steadied herself on Minno. Then she stretched out as far as she could. Her fingertips barely pressed at the lever. She pushed, swallowing an agonizing grunt.

Nothing happened.

"Those Ooglys are gonna sniff us out," Hailey warned, exasperated.

"Oh, like I wouldn't have figured that out," Minno shot back.

Tears filled Minno's eyes. She swallowed as much of the pain as she could.

"I'm just saying ..." Hailey added.

"Push harder, please. My arm's going numb."

Hailey pushed with everything she had left—still nothing.

Minno's pain doubled in that moment. She wanted to scream, but she knew that meant certain capture and failure. She had to hold on. Think! There had to be a way to get free.

"I can't get it," Hailey whispered. She was on the verge of tears herself.

"You have to. Believe you can do it, and you will do it," Minno said, trying to inspire her friend. They needed more than just inspiration.

Minno worked her bag off her shoulder, handed it to Hailey.

"Wrap the bag around the lever. We both pull at once."

Hailey wasted no time, nor effort, getting the bag in place. Once done, she slid down to rest beside Minno with the straps in both their hands.

Pain clawed into Minno's head, hazing her thinking while sizzling down her spine.

"Pull," Minno commanded.

Both girls pulled the bag straps. The lever moved, slowly at first, then just enough to release Minno's arm. The bar slid out of the lock.

Success! The lock dropped open with a jolt.

But when it did, the girls spilled out the keyhole and onto the floor. They gazed up to a circle of soldiers surrounding them.

"Guess we didn't think that through," Hailey offered.

The open lock still held the chains intact across the doors. If only one chain slipped off, the doors could open. But how could the girls even attempt to move such huge doors by themselves?

The soldiers made no move to close in; instead, they peeled back so Craveaux and the Ooglys could reach the girls. The high minister's sinister smile sent chills up the girls' spines. He had them. But neither Minno nor Hailey were about to surrender without a fight.

They scrambled to their feet. Backing into the lock to keep distance between them and Craveaux, they caused a chain to slip. It inched closer to coming off.

"Foolish little girls," the high minister said with a whimsy in his voice. They were his prisoners now. There was nothing they could do to change what was about to happen. Craveaux stared at the bag clutched in Minno's hand. All the power in the kingdom would be his.

The high minister lunged, and in one smooth swipe, ripped the bag from Minno's grip.

"No!" Minno screamed.

"I'm a graceful ballerina!" Gutty's voice rang out from somewhere high up in the darkness looming over the dungeon.

Minno and Hailey searched. There he was!

Gutty, all glorious nine feet of him, sailed in from a high ledge. But he crashed not onto the soldiers—but rather into the giant lock. His jarring action allowed the chain to slip off the lock arm and clank to the floor.

"You're free!" he yelled as loud as he could.

For one tense, unending moment nothing in the dungeon dared to move. Not a single soldier raised his sword, nor a single Oogly brother lunged for the girls. Silence filled the air.

Then came wild flapping from behind the great doors.

Gutty tossed two soldiers into the Oogly brothers.

Screaming, chaos and pandemonium took over! The first surge of dragon flesh crashed against the giant doors, forcing them to peel open before soldiers could throw their collective weight against them. Raucous dragon screeching drowned out the cries of soldiers fleeing in every possible direction.

"Gutty! You're alive!" Hailey screamed in joy.

But the girls had no time to enjoy a reunion with the huge troll. Minno went after her bag, while Hailey attacked Moogly, throwing punches and kicks to force the Oogly back into the soldiers.

"Ha! I saw that on TV!" she yelled, driving a fist into Moogly's chest.

Moogly counterattacked, slinging wild, feminine slaps—exactly the way a girl would fight.

"God, you fight like a girl!"

"I am a girl," Moogly retorted, offended.

"Whoa, didn't see that comin'." Hailey grabbed Moogly's collar to jerk her to the floor.

The burgeoning dragon flesh took over the entire dungeon. Dragons flapped wildly in any attempt to take flight in the confining conditions.

Craveaux knocked Minno away, keeping control of the bag while at the same moment folding into the chaos. But Minno yanked the high minister's robe to spin him back to face her.

"Oh, no you don't. That's my bag," she said.

Minno clamped onto the bag, tugging with all her strength.

Craveaux threw back an arm to deliver a blue lightning bolt. But at that moment a dragon lurched forward striking the arm. The lightning bolt missed, ricocheting off the rock walls. Dragons dodged and swooped to avoid the burning light. Soldiers dove for the floor, covering heads.

Minno snatched her bag back!

The high minister had to retreat. He slipped out empty-handed amongst the fleeing soldiers. In another moment he was gone, along with the soldiers and the fleeing dragons.

The dungeon became strangely silent.

Hailey hugged Gutty's leg, her arms barely reaching around.

Uncertain of how to react, Gutty simply patted her head.

"You missed me!" Gutty said surprised.

"Of course, I missed you," Hailey responded.

"Gutty, it's so good you're alive!" Minno added.

Gutty just smiled. He vaulted his egg horn for them to see.

"Told you ... good luck."

"I really, really missed you, big guy. Don't go dying again, yo-kay?"

"Yo-kay," he replied to Hailey. Then he leaned down to Minno.

"I promised your mother nothing would happen to you. We need to go now."

"Not yet. There's one more thing we need to do," Minno said with a hard defiance in her eyes. Their fight was not over yet. And it wouldn't be until she finished it. She had one more task to accomplish before evacuating the fortress.

Gutty knew in that moment there was no changing Minno's mind.

"What?" Hailey chimed in. "You said free the dragons and get out of here. Now you're changing your mind? I can't believe ..." she ranted until Minno silenced her with a raised finger. She would not be deterred by her friend.

"We've come this far. We finish it here and now. We're gonna make sure Craveaux can't hurt Gutty or any other creatures anymore."

"Yo-kay," both Gutty and Hailey replied in unison.

With that Gutty led them into a darkened tunnel.

33

Outside in the market square, beneath the blaring sun, the first free dragons surged through the palace doors, taking flight above fleeing soldiers and scurrying peasants. Terrified screams saturated the air. Bodies pushed this way and that, desperate to avoid the scaly beasts.

The cacophony jarred a sleeping Nole awake. He had hours earlier fallen dead asleep while approaching the palace doors near an out-of-the-way alcove. He sprang to his feet, thrashing wildly, punching only air. Then he realized what was happening. A dragon's wing flapped past him on its way upward.

"She did it!" his voice rang out louder than it should have. His words caught a young, bushy-haired soldier's attention.

"Run!" the armed youth cried.

Nole tripped the young man, so as he fell, the troll hunter could relieve him of his sword.

"You'll not need this. Now hurry and escape before it is too late."

The young soldier scrambled to his feet and scampered away, refusing to fight Nole for the blade.

As Nole watched, Sachea and Antinarra breached the fortress gates leading the Forbit clan and a band of trolls. The Forbits spread out to attack the oncoming soldiers spilling into the crowded square.

Swords clanked back and forth, jamming the soldiers back toward the palace doors.

Nole parted fleeing peasants to gain a path into the palace through the now sheared-off doors.

The Forbit clan cleared a path at the gates wide enough to allow the trolls to surge through. The trolls, by their sheer ten-foot size would keep the soldiers from overrunning the Forbits. Since trolls and Forbits would have never entered the fortress on their own, this was the first time the Palladins faced so many creatures head on. Before, trolls only entered through the gates in chains and at the charge of a troll hunter.

Terrified Palladins scattered in all directions. Some were able to skirt the onrush of trolls to slip out the fortress gates before a charging troll could grab them.

What the Palladins failed to comprehend in all the ensuing pandemonium was that the Forbit clan and the trolls only sought to frighten the Palladins into fleeing. Neither had any desire to harm them.

The trolls swiped at the fleeing Palladins, missing intentionally by wide margins, thereby ensuring not a single peasant might be harmed, as long as the Palladins harmed none of them.

34

In the dark bowels of the fortress, Minno entered the power chamber to stand before the huge spinning rock pulsating with its green glow. Hailey and Gutty remained in the corridor.

"You're kidding, right?" Hailey asked, uncertain of what response she might get.

"That's impossible," Gutty added. He stared in amazement at the object that was to be the cause of his death. The troll couldn't comprehend any of it: The glowing rock, the hoses and pipes, and more importantly, how Minno might think she could destroy such a huge powerful object.

"Thanks for being so positive. Besides, I've got the bag, remember." However, Minno's voice lacked sufficient conviction to convince even her. At the moment she had no plan whatsoever.

While Minno gazed at the power stone, the chamber doors slammed closed behind her. Hailey's scream squirmed through the crack. Minno knew she was in trouble.

"This is between Craveaux and the Soma," came from the side of the power chamber beyond her view.

Minno's skin crawled. She swallowed hard. The moment of her destiny had arrived. She turned to face her nemesis.

A blue lightning bolt fired across her bow.

Craveaux fired it not at her, but rather into a statue flanking the doors. It toppled into the other and together the statues blocked the door shut. Then he emerged into the green glow of the spinning power stone.

"I'm not afraid of you," Minno offered, holding her fear in check long enough to get the words out without revealing her true apprehension.

The high minister turned back to Minno. His eye sockets peered deep into hers, drilling into her soul to assess the conviction of her statement. He detected no fear in her ... yet.

"You will be," he replied plainly. His face shifted from hers to her dragon-wing bag. His power necklace pulsed virulent green.

"Do you know who scarred my face—who took my eyes?"

Minno said nothing.

"Your precious Desrilian."

Craveaux fired another sizzling blue lightning bolt.

Minno angled her bag, successfully deflecting the strike. The lightning bolt angled off the bag, ricocheted off the stone floor then bounced off the nearest wall. It found the glowing rock. The huge spinning orb wobbled, its disturbance rippling through the entire fortress like a small earthquake. Everything around them was inexorably linked to the great power stone.

Craveaux swallowed hard. He realized he had underestimated this little girl and her powerful bag. But worse, he had disrupted the delicate balance of the power stone.

C-r-a-c-k!

The situation moved from serious to critical mass when two stone pillars supporting the spinning rock fractured.

"I have underestimated you," he said. His smile disappeared. His face turned as cold and as hard as the power stone spinning at their flank.

"Yeah. I'm way tougher than I look," Minno bragged.

"*Not you.* The bag."

The errant lightning bolt had set off a chain of events Craveaux had not counted on. The pipes and hoses circling the great rock shuddered loudly. Then they began to crack. Though only small cracks at first appeared, within moments, the cracks grew long and wide, sending shards of crude pipe raining down around them.

The chamber walls and ceiling succumbed in turn. Craveaux's fortress, his long impregnable sanctuary from the creatures beyond its walls, began to falter.

The high minister attacked, knocking Minno down with a wide swipe of his arm before stripping her of the bag.

"You're nothing but a little nuisance," he jabbed, feeling the smooth leather in his fingers and the bag's power flowing up his arms. Nothing else would matter now that he had the dragon wing. All power in Ambrosia belonged to him. He would seize whatever he wished. No one would dare oppose him, as long as he held Desrilian's dragon wing.

"Desrilian also thought he could defeat me. I destroyed a king to have this," he said. "The dragons were fools to trust a Palladin."

Triumphant, Craveaux turned to leave. But the statue blocked the door. He readied another lightning bolt to clear the way.

Minno's hand yanked him back.

"You're not going anywhere with my bag."

The high minister took pause.

"Do you honestly think I will fall to a *little girl*?" he taunted.

Minno lunged as Craveaux whirled about, his flailing arm knocking her back down. Then an overhead pipe fractured, releasing a hissing mist cloud above their heads.

Craveaux became disoriented, thrashing wildly and desperately ... like he was attempting to swim through the mist cloud blindly while fending her off. But the mist hovered two feet above them.

Minno realized at that moment what it meant. Frantically, she searched the room. That had to be the answer.

There they were!

The mist revealed the high minister's green glowing eyes floating overhead.

"Ha! I got you now, Craveaux!" Minno spat out his name with disdain. She sprang to her feet, groping the surrounding floor. Locating a length of fallen stone pipe, Minno attacked not Craveaux—but his eyes. Her wild slashing forced the eyes to bob and weave, which sent the high minister into crazy, uncoordinated gyrations, like a person desperate to escape a bee in his pants. With his eyes ducking and bouncing so fervently to avoid Minno's swings, Craveaux could no longer keep his balance, let alone attack her.

But those eyes were adept at bobbing and floating, so for all her effort, Minno accomplished no more harm than to keep Craveaux disoriented.

"Stop! I can't take it anymore," the high minister cried out, steadying his head with his hands. The room spun in ever faster concentric circles. He needed to stand still to regain his equilibrium before dizziness took him from his feet.

In the next moment, Minno ripped the bag back with one hand, while swiping at the eyes with the other. She had to keep him disoriented long enough to escape.

Craveaux took to flailing like a wild man, firing blue lightning bolts everywhere, hoping one might strike Minno. All missed. But one did nail the huge stone, along with its forward facing supports. The closest support gave way, forcing Minno to abandon the eyes in favor of dodging huge quartz chunks cascading down to crush her.

In the next moment the mist faded, the eyes disappeared into the green glow. Craveaux stumbled away, going for the door.

"Oh, no, I'm not done with you yet, bucko!" Minno said, rummaging for a replacement staff.

The high minister regained his composure, spun about to face Minno while he readied his arm for another lightning bolt strike.

"Craveaux will have the dragon wing."

He threw his arm back, fired another glowing bolt!

But this one fizzled, too weak to inflict pain. It buzzed to the floor a few feet short of reaching Minno.

"Uh, oh," was all Craveaux could eek out in response.

Minno leapt over stone chunks, performing a front flip to land a dozen paces before the high minister.

The glowing stone wobbled out of control now. The mighty power Craveaux once wielded against the creatures of Ambrosia had deteriorated into a fizzle and a pop.

The ceiling split apart. Cracks crawled the walls, widening as they ascended. The overhead quartz opened in the center; shards of glass rock rained down around them.

A fissure opened in the rear wall allowing blinding sunlight in.

Craveaux's power necklace was all but extinguished.

Minno had him now. All she need do is force him to surrender. But no worthy victory would come that easy. She measured a six-foot length of pipe across her hands.

"You're going down, Craveaux. This is for Gutty, my parents, and all the creatures you've hurt." Minno's voice remained calm, measured. She wore an expression of resolve. She was no longer afraid, nor was she excited. She came to realize who she was and the role she must play in this place. She would do what she must do to save the creatures of Ambrosia. One of them would leave here the victor, the other the vanquished. Minno had no intention of accepting the latter.

A part of her expected Craveaux to flee like a frightened sixth grader. After all, his power had been crushed, and she wore hers over her shoulder. He had to know at this point he'd never take what was rightfully hers.

But the high minister refused to back down. He charged with a pipe of his own. He was taller and stronger, so he thought he might relieve her of her bag and still escape the fortress before it totally collapsed.

Clanking pipe against pipe, they battled back and forth, edging closer to the wobbling stone. Initially, Craveaux held the advantage, forcing Minno nearer the open fissure. But at the last second, she sidestepped, swung at another overhead pipe.

She missed it!

Her tactical move only made the high minister laugh.

"You're out of tricks, *little girl*," he taunted.

"I told you, don't ... call ... me ... little ... girl."

She rushed him, which was exactly what he wanted. But she leapt onto a fallen stone support to slash another overhead pipe.

It fractured!

A mist cloud drifted overhead.

Craveaux tried to fight in earnest, but his vision caused him trouble. He lowered his pipe into a jousting position and charged, seeking to take Minno through the open fissure.

Minno spun, slid sideways, where she slashed at his pipe as he closed in. Craveaux's momentum carried him against his will. As he surged past, Minno threw a leg out to trip him.

Craveaux stumbled through the open fissure, abandoning his pipe as he tumbled into blinding daylight. The high minister clung to a rock jutting out from the wall, as forty feet below, his pipe stabbed the rushing river.

For a moment Minno remained in the background, watching the high minister dangle. Should she just allow him to fall? It would serve him right for all the pain he caused the creatures of Ambrosia. Certainly any creature in her position would turn their back to flee the fortress before it completely caved in. But would that then make her like Craveaux? Would she have become the same kind of person as he?

At first she couldn't decide.

The high minister struggled with a single hand clinging in the fissure. He gazed down at the river—an army of fish gathered, waiting to attack.

Minno's hand came through.

"Take it," she said.

"Never," Craveaux responded at first.

The wall cracked further. Another fissure opened a few feet away, allowing the rock outcropping aiding the high minister to droop further away from the wall.

"Your fortress is coming apart. It's over, Craveaux. Give up. Take my hand. You can live peacefully with all the creatures here. The dragons will agree."

Craveaux listened. A sudden brainstorm swept into his head.

"Please, you're right. Don't let me die. I don't want to die," he cried.

"Then take my hand."

"I can't. I might slip. Use your bag. Your bag will save me."

Without thinking, and because she knew the bag would provide Craveaux something to cling to until she could work him safely back inside, Minno extended the bag out the fissure for the high minister.

The high minister smiled.

Minno realized her mistake ... but it was too late.

Craveaux's fist tightened around the bag. His sinister smile beamed up at her.

"Let go," Minno said.

He laughed.

"Foolish *little girl*. It's mine now."

The high minister released his hold on the rock outcropping, fully expecting to tumble into the river below with the precious bag in hand.

But the bag held fast, which only angered Craveaux further.

He reached in to snare Minno's collar, using it to jerk her out of the fissure. She latched onto the rock outcropping for dear life.

"Release the bag, I let you live," he said.

"Not a chance."

Minno ripped the bag from his hand. She followed that with a solid fist to his chest.

Craveaux's grip faltered. He couldn't hang on. He took one last wild swipe at the bag as he fell away from Minno.

"I told you, no one gets my bag," Minno called to him.

She clung to the fissure with one hand, while clutching her bag in the other. Her grip slipped when she tried to bring her second hand back up to take hold. Her fingers ached. All the strength in her arms had fled. She had only a few seconds before . . .

"Grab hold. I'll bring you back in," a Scottish voice said from inside.

Minno gazed up into the red eyes of the huge rat looking down at her. It extended its right foreleg to within her reach.

"Trust me," the rat said.

35

Gutty rammed the doors. At first they held. Then they gave way a little, allowing Hailey to see the statue blocking them closed. She studied the situation for a moment.

"Push real hard on this door," she instructed Gutty, indicating the one on the right.

"You gotta force it open, Gutty. We have to save her."

With a groan so loud and powerful that one might have thought the sound alone would move the door, Gutty complied. The statue screeched back further into the power chamber. The door yielded enough for Hailey to squeeze through.

As Hailey climbed over the statue's arm, the remaining power stone supports crashed in on each other causing a cloud of dust and debris. The ceiling toppled in near the power stone.

"Minno!" she screamed above the rumble of the fortress coming apart.

Sunlight streamed in from the fissure, permeating the dust cloud consuming the room. Hailey coughed to clear her throat while groping the rubble all around her. Minno was nowhere in sight.

Then a hand grabbed the top of the quartz rubble, followed by a silhouette rising to the top of the heap. Through the dust Hailey could only discern that it was a person.

Then the silhouette placed the bag over her shoulder. Minno blocked out the blinding sun while emerging from the dust cloud.

Hailey threw her arms around her, hugging Minno tightly. A moment later she let her go.

"Let's go home," Minno said, throwing an arm over her friend's shoulder.

They dodged ceiling chunks, scrambling from the power chamber to meet up with Gutty in the corridor.

"You're safe now," he told Minno, placing his hand on her shoulder.

"*We're* safe now," she corrected

"Not until we're out of here," Hailey added.

They raced down the corridor then up a winding staircase that had cracked down the center. At the top they entered a vaulted open chamber. There they stopped.

Soldiers amassed across from them. A dozen swords fell into line to run them through if they advanced further.

"Now what?" Hailey asked, looking at Minno in terror.

Minno removed her bag, yet she had no idea how she might use it against the soldiers.

"This way!" Nole called from the side of the chamber.

He leveled his sword against the soldiers.

Hailey did some quick math.

"Twelve against one," she said.

"Yes, but I have a sword now," Nole replied with a smile so large and bold that one would have thought the troll hunter held the advantage over the soldiers.

The soldiers, however, refused to back down as Nole advanced into the chamber.

"Behind me," the troll hunter commanded.

"I'm thinking we should come up with a better plan than that," Hailey said.

As the soldiers closed in, Nole slashed wildly from side to side to protect the girls and Gutty. The soldiers relented, backing them all slowly against the wall until there was no place left to retreat.

"This isn't working!" Hailey yelled above clamoring steel.

"They're falling right into my trap," Nole corrected.

"That's what you said back at Yapper valley," Gutty offered.

Scrambling along the floor, Hailey recovered a fallen sword. She tossed it to Minno.

"What do you expect me to do with this?"

"I figured you knew how to use it," Hailey replied.

"Well, I don't," Minno said.

"Great. Your grandpa never taught you how to fight with a sword?"

"No."

Just then the Forbit clan bounced in from nowhere, leveling swords between Nole and the soldiers. Commander Dulfay led the clan into the foray. In moments the tide of the battle reversed.

"You didn't think you were alone in this, did you?" Dulfay said while slashing at an advancing soldier. "We'll hold them off. You get clear."

The Forbits surged with swords flailing, forcing the soldiers to retreat step by step, thus creating a clear path for Nole, Gutty and the girls to escape.

"Fortune go with you," Dulfay yelled.

But as he spoke his concentration faltered. A soldier's blade sliced into Dulfay's soft white belly. Blood gushed as Dulfay struck down the soldier.

"Dulfay!" Minno yelled in agony at the sight of the commander crumpling to his knees. His sword clattered against the stone floor. His eyes went wide with disbelief.

"Fulfill your destiny," Dulfay said.

Then he was gone.

Nole covered their backs as the girls and Gutty dashed through an archway that spilled into the kitchen, where more soldiers were organizing. But they never got the chance to advance on the girls. Dragons swooped in from high in the timber rafters.

"Retreat!" a soldier yelled, launching his sword futilely at a descending beast before scampering out.

A frantic barrage of arrows and spears flew unaimed at the beasts. The dragons' screeching alone terrified all those present.

Crystal chunks fell into the grand hall, crushing the ornate chair Craveaux used to preside over his underlings. Gutty led the girls through a current of men, women and children escaping the crumbling walls.

A six-year-old little girl in tattered clothes with matted dark hair and grimy face stumbled into Hailey's feet. Hailey quickly snatched her up and they ran together.

"Keep hold of my hand. I'll get you to safety," Hailey said to calm the terror in the child's eyes.

"How much further?" Minno asked over the noisy crowd. It was the first time her confidence seemed shaken.

"Almost there," Gutty reassured her.

They exited the grand hall to disappear into another corridor.

At the end of the hall Minno could see the daylight as people spilled through the doors into the market square.

Hailey emerged first, coughing out dust, still clinging to the little girl's hand. Then came Minno, cradling a young boy in both her arms, and finally came Gutty, clutching a child in each of his arms.

When they looked up into the sky, they could see dragons circling the fortress. Occasionally one swooped in at soldiers trying to fight them off. To their left, a trio of trolls tossed onrushing soldiers every which way like bean bags. Though the trolls were outnumbered twenty-to-one, they fought through the armed men toward the fortress doors, some taking arrows to their torsos but refusing to yield.

"Hey, those are my cousins," Gutty chimed, waving so they would see him. The trolls briefly stopped their assault, waving back and smiling.

Then Sickly emerged. He skirted around Gutty and the girls to reach the open center of the square.

"Craveaux has fallen. Save yourselves!" Sickly announced with all the strength he could muster, which was little for a man of advanced years.

But the words themselves turned the tides of the battle raging between the creatures of Ambrosia and the soldiers in the square. The dragons and the trolls ceased their assault, allowing the soldiers and the peasants to flee. Hailey, Gutty and Minno released the children to their terrified yet grateful parents, who fled with the others.

Within minutes all the Palladins had fled ... except for Nole. He lowered his sword, going to Antinarra, who stood armed with a sword watching their enemies abandon the fight.

"Not all Palladins are evil," he said to her.

She turned a skeptical eye.

"Perhaps you are right."

They banded together in the market square to walk to the destroyed fortress gates. As the Palladins scattered into the fields and the forest, the vegetation surrounding the fortress sprang back to life, sprouting green and tall to blanket the lifeless dirt with new birth.

Overhead, dragons circled, not to attack, but rather to defend the creatures below.

"You saved them, Minno. You saved us all," Gutty vaulted.

The trolls behind Gutty cheered while plucking arrows from their chests like porcupine quills.

"Ya-hoo!" Hailey cheered.

"Ya-hoo!" everyone else cheered in unison, though no one had any idea what the word meant.

Hailey and Minno shared a high-five. When Gutty put out his hand, neither responded. His face turned sullen. Minno took his hand, high-fived him.

"*We* did it," she said.

But her words brought sadness to Gutty's face. His sadness infected Minno and Hailey.

"That means you're gonna leave now," Gutty said.

The moment hung between them. Gutty's words tugged at their hearts. Neither girl spoke. They would have to leave Gutty behind and return to their world. Worst of all, Minno would have to leave her parents. She needed to return to Blue Lake and hope her grandpa had somehow escaped the Arachnorock Craveaux had sent through after them.

"I'm not leaving," Hailey blurted out suddenly, surprising Minno and Gutty. "My essence, it's here now. I have people here." A stern resolve laced her voice.

"He's a troll ... not exactly people," Minno corrected.

"I don't care. I go back through that portal I could lose my voice," Hailey added in defense of her decision.

"You've got to be kidding me," Minno said.

"No. I'm dead serious," Hailey replied.

"Not that," Minno corrected, "*that!*"

She pointed.

In the open field preceding the forest's fringe, Craveaux rode in a crystalline enclosed carriage, carried by four Goggs wearing wide silver Choggas. These fierce-looking rhinoceros-like creatures marched upright with tough leather-skinned bodies and elephantine feet. Hundreds of mounted soldiers surrounded the high minister as they raced away from the fortress.

"It is only just beginning, isn't it?" Gutty asked.

"*What* is only just beginning?" Minno asked, unsure of what Gutty meant.

"The war," Nole added absently. His eyes never left the sight of Craveaux escaping.

Minno looked at him.

"On which side do you stand, Palladin?" Antinarra asked.

Her question brought Nole's eyes to hers. She read his answer there. Her heart fluttered, even though they were creatures from opposing worlds.

Nole brought his blade up.

"I pledge my blade, my life, to the ..."

Before the troll hunter could finish, he crumpled into Antinarra's arms, his sword dropped into the dirt, and there he began snoring.

"Good grief, not again," Antinarra said, lowering him to her feet.

Minno gazed off to the horizon. She understood what it all meant now. She knew why her grandfather had worked with her so hard back in Blue Lake. She realized the role she must play in this land she came from but never knew. She believed in what was now her destiny. Her parents would need her to keep them safe from Craveaux.

They were not done.

"Yeah," Hailey pondered. "What? The war? What war?"

Regardless of what the future held, Hailey knew she belonged here, and oddly enough, she belonged with Gutty. Yet she couldn't bring to words why she felt the way she felt about him. She hugged his leg and offered him a smile, which he returned in kind.

"I think we're gonna need a lot more of my cousins to help with this one," Gutty offered.

Sachea swooped in, landing before Gutty and the girls. Antinarra in turn left Nole to join Minno, while another dragon, this one larger than Sachea, Osomoray by name, glided in to land before Minno. This dragon's scales were a verdant green, darker than the others, which made the distinguishing yellow diamond on its forehead more prominent.

"Dad?" Minno said. She knew in her heart at that moment she was standing before her father. At first she couldn't fathom why she knew. Then she realized she had seen the yellow diamond on a colored-pencil drawing her grandfather had shown her so many years ago.

"You have your mother's eyes," Osomoray said.

"Daddy!" Minno chimed. The way he looked at her with teary eyes confirmed it in Minno's heart and mind.

"I have missed you dearly, Minnovera," he added.

A swarm of nymphflies hovered over Sachea's head as they awaited instructions.

"Convey to all in the land that Craveaux has fled his fortress. Our day of reckoning has at last arrived," Sachea said.

As soon as she finished speaking, the nymphflies began producing bubbles—thousands of bubbles that drifted skyward to disperse in all directions. Soon all the creatures who once feared the evil tyrant would know the significance of this day, and would fear him no longer, for outside his once mighty fortress, the high minister was vulnerable to their magic.

The Forbit clan, the trolls, the dragons and all the other strange creatures of Ambrosia came together to surround the girls. In moments their numbers grew into the hundreds, all crowding before the fallen fortress.

"All cheer the Soma!" a Forbit called out, vaulting his sword toward the pristine sky. His entire clan followed suit.

The roar of gratitude from the creatures of Ambrosia reverberated throughout the entire valley beyond the fortress. Minno was certain even Craveaux would have heard it, and now knew his reign of terror was no more.

One of the Forbits carried a large pot on his back with three Patsche in it. The Patsche stretched out tall, waving back and forth.

"Huzzah!" a Patsche said.

"I say, good show," another called out.

"Desrilian must be proud of you. You have done a fine job," Osomoray said to Minno.

"It saddens us greatly, but we must let you return home. Craveaux will do everything in his power to get his hands on you and the dragon wi..." Sachea said.

Before Sachea could finish, a black silver-banded hummingbird swooped in to hover close to Minno.

"This is not over, little girl! Craveaux has something you want ..." the bird said, mimicking Craveaux's voice exactly.

Then, as if in the background, came an agonizing scream— Grandpa Esri's scream.

"Minno, don't listen to him. You must *not* come for me. You must not ri ..." Esri's tortured voice continued through the mouth of the hummingbird until something silenced it.

"And you have something Craveaux wants ... the dragon wing. Bring it to Mortus within two cycles of the moon, or your precious Desrilian dies!" Craveaux's voice cut back in.

Minno looked at Hailey—Hailey stared back at Minno. A thrill beyond comprehension coursed through Minno's veins. Grandpa Esri was alive! But now they could not leave this place until her grandfather was once again safe.

The end ... or merely the beginning ....